I0726914

ESCAPE FROM KUFA

In the Name of God, the Kind, the Merciful. All praise is for God alone, Lord of all the worlds, and may the peace and blessings of God be showered on the Holy Prophet and his Household.
To my beloved teacher who showed me how to live and how to worship before he returned back to his Lord. To my incredible parents for their constant prayers and advice. Thank you Shaykh Mohammad Saeed Bahmanpour for checking the work for historical accuracy. To Fatma Ali Jaffer for the excellent edits and constant encourgament. To Maryam MJ for proofreading.
May Allah (swt) reward you beyond your expectations.

ESCAPE FROM KUFA

Published by
Sun Behind The Cloud Publications Ltd
PO Box 15889, Birmingham, B16 6NZ
This first editon published in paperback in 2023
©Sun Behind The Cloud Publications
The moral right of the author has been asserted
All rights reserved
A CIP catalogue of this book is available from The British Library.
ISBN (Print): 978-1-908110-90-9

www.sunbehindthecloud.com
info@sunbehindthecloud.com
Instagram: @sunbehindcloud
Facebook: @sunbehindthecloud

فَخَرَجَ مِنْهَا خَآئِفًا يَتَرَقَّبُ قَالَ رَبِّ نَجِّنِى مِنَ ٱلْقَوْمِ ٱلظَّـٰلِمِينَ

So he left the city in a state of fear and caution, praying,
"My Lord! Deliver me from the wrongdoing people."

وَلَمَّا تَوَجَّهَ تِلْقَآءَ مَدْيَنَ قَالَ عَسَىٰ رَبِّى أَن يَهْدِيَنِى سَوَآءَ ٱلسَّبِيلِ

And as he made his way towards Midian, he said,
"I trust my Lord will guide me to the right way."

Surah al Qasas, verse 21-22

DISCLAIMER

This book is based in the city of Kufa in the year 61 A.H. Every effort has been made to use authentic sources when referencing the historical context or any speech of the Imams and work has been checked by scholars for historical accuracy. However, Zayd and his uncle Haarith are fictional characters and Zayd's escape from Kufa is entirely fictional. It is reported that some followers of the Ahlulbayt (as) did try to escape from Kufa to join Imam Husayn (as) and fight on the Day of Ashura; the most famous of these was Habib ibn Mazahir.

May Allah (swt) grant us a love for Imam Husayn (as) that motivates us to improve ourselves and may He make us enter heaven with the Ahlulbayt (as).

READ THIS FIRST

What you are about to read is not just a story. It is a quest for the truth and a challenge to test your resourcefulness and creativity. If you choose to accept it, you will embark on an adventure through threatening confrontations, underground tunnels and landscapes full of predators. Do you have the courage and ingenuity to reach the final goal?

Zayd realises that Imam Husayn is in danger. He cannot leave his Imam alone in his time of need. But how can he escape the clutches of his uncle and make it through the treacherous alleys of a Kufa under curfew before dawn? He is only fifteen years old and he has never done anything like this before. He needs your help!

As you journey with Zayd, read each chapter until you reach this symbol.

When you get there, solve the code or puzzle that follows in order to progress to the next chapter. The solution to each puzzle will provide you with a number indicating the page number that you need to turn to if you are to continue the journey.

Read the chapters carefully and use your skills of observation and analysis to help Zayd escape Kufa and join Imam Husayn.

Good luck, give it your best shot!

P.S. If you get stuck along the way, there are clues and solutions at the end of the book for all the puzzles and codes.

THE CELLAR

Zayd's body lies on the cold cellar floor. His eyes are closed. A blow to the head has dishevelled his once neatly wrapped turban and a bruise is beginning to form where he was struck. The coarse material of his shirt is sticky with the blood from the lacerations on his back.

His chest rises and falls weakly. His eyelids flicker. He opens his eyes for a moment – long enough to see the shadowy figure of his uncle disappear as the cellar door slams shut. A moment of silence follows and then he hears the scraping of the bolt and the click of the heavy lock. A few more seconds of quiet – is his uncle having second thoughts? – before the sound of determined footsteps, echoing clearly at first and then slowly fading away until nothing but an eerie silence remains.

A single tear falls down Zayd's cheek marking a path on his sore, dust-encrusted cheek.

****

Zayd both loves and hates his uncle. After Zayd's father had been killed by Muawiya, Haarith had married his mother and taken them both in. Although they have their differences – Zayd's young blood bubbles in frustration at his uncle's indifference to the Ahlulbayt – he has always been kind to Zayd. But Haarith never seems to take him seriously, always seeing him as just a boy missing his father.

Tonight was different.

I forbid you to leave!

Haarith had put his foot down.

Enough is enough!

Perhaps it was the spark of defiance in Zayd's eyes that had agitated him.

How dare you? After everything I have done.

Zayd knew that Haarith was worried not just for him, but for the rest of the tribe as well. His words and actions could put them in a lot of danger. After all, Muslim ibn Aqeel's body was hanging from the city gates as a warning to anyone considering taking the side of Husayn ibn Ali. The people of Kufa who had once supported their Imam had now turned their backs on him, but Zayd could not.

"Uncle," Zayd pleaded earlier as they sat for their evening meal. "Husayn ibn Ali is on his way to Kufa. You know they will not let him reach here safely. What if they attack him in the middle of the desert? He is the son of Ali and Fatimah! How can we sit at home and do nothing to help him?"

The first blow to the face took Zayd by surprise and he fell to the ground with a crash, spilling a jug of white laban all over the floor. Zayd was stunned equally by the force of the knock and surprise that his uncle had struck him. He felt a metallic taste on his tongue and rubbed his mouth with the back of his hand. It came away with a dark smear of blood.

"You foolish boy!" Haarith yelled. "Can you really think this is as simple a matter as that? Do you know what it means to get involved in a dispute between Husayn ibn Ali and the Caliph? It has nothing to do with us and the Caliph will destroy us!"

"But don't you understand, Uncle? Husayn is not an ordinary man, he is our Imam! He must be respected, followed...obeyed!"

"Didn't you hear what Ibn Ziyad said?"

Zayd knew well the ominous words that had been whispered in the alleys from one house to another across Kufa: *My whip and my sword shall strike anyone who disobeys my command.* But what was a worldly threat when compared to the duty he owed to the Prophet's grandson?

"My father was not frightened of these bullies," Zayd's voice rose as he slowly got back to his feet. "And neither am I!" He stood up straight and faced his uncle with a determined look.

"Your father was an idiot who got himself killed!" spat out Haarith.

The words echoed between Zayd's ears, matching the throbbing pain that was rhythmically drumming in his head. He closed his eyes for a second to gather his thoughts and carefully wiped his wound with the loose end of his turban. "My father was killed supporting Imam Hasan," he bit out through clenched teeth. "And I will give my life for Husayn!"

Zayd turned on his heel and made his way out of the house. He strode to the gate of their courtyard and began to bridle his horse. The animal, sensing the tension in the air, was restless and as Zayd tried to calm him down, he didn't notice that his uncle had followed him out of the house.

Haarith seized the bridle from Zayd's hand and grabbed him in a chokehold.

"I have heard enough from you!" he growled. "You are a stubborn brat who is intent on leading our entire family to destruction!"

Haarith dragged Zayd back to the house and down into the cellar.

"It's time you got a taste of what Ibn Ziyad has threatened! It might bring you to your senses!"

****

Zayd focuses his energy on breathing. In...out....in...out... Once his heart is beating at a steady pace, he carefully pushes himself up on his knees. A deep groan escapes him; every inch of his body protests against the movement. He waits a few moments and then takes another deep breath and pushes himself up on his elbows. Now on all fours, he scans the cellar like a wounded animal weary of its predator.

His position of semi-sujood reminds him of that night a month ago when he had prayed behind Muslim ibn Aqeel, Imam Husayn's cousin and messenger to Kufa. How Ibn Ziyad's arrival has changed everything!

Slowly, his disorientation dissipates. The memory of the treacherous betrayal of the Kufans to Muslim fuels him and his heart beats with force once again. His thoughts turn to Imam Husayn and his heart shatters. Imam Husayn will be stopped by Kufan soldiers for sure and then what will they do? Threaten him?

Harm him? *God Forbid!* Zayd falters at the thought and dread weighs heavily on him. He lowers his head in resignation, tears falling freely from his eyes as he sits on his knees, shoulders slumped, and all strength drained from him. How can he do anything to help his Imam while stuck in this stone prison? He might as well be dead and buried!

What would Father do? The thought comes unbidden as it often has at those times in his life when he has an important decision to make. His father has been his inspiration and role model. What would *he* do?

Zayd knows the answer. It is reflected in both the life and death that his father chose and resonates with what his heart is telling him from deep within. He cannot stay here. He must join Imam Husayn. There is no time to waste. ESCAPE! The word is clear in his mind. He must find a way out of this cellar and advance without delay.

It is difficult to see in the small, featureless room. Zayd feels around with his hands, searching for anything out of place that might suggest a way out. This cellar has been a frequent hideout to escape chores; he will not let it become his prison. He knows it is bare. A desert owl hoots from a distance away and Zayd realises that the sound is clearer than it should be below ground. He licks the tips of his fingers and raises his arm as high as he can. A draft! There is definitely a cool breeze coming into the room! But there is no a window in this room...

He takes a few deep breaths. The air is fresh but also filled with the scent of wet earth. Suddenly a fissure of excitement runs down his spine. His uncle has been complaining that a collapsed gutter has damaged a portion of the outer wall at street level and is letting air into the house. Is it possible that this hole has broken into the ceiling of the cellar?

Zayd begins to walk along the wall, hands pressed against it, sniffing with every step and praying desperately. *"Allahu Akbar!"* The words escape his lips as his fingers come across a damp patch. He scrapes at it and when the mud crumbles under his fingers, he feels his heart expand. A way out! Hope!

If he can make holes in the mud wall to serve as handholds and footholds, he can reach up and widen the damaged hole into the street. Freedom is within his reach. His muscles tense. Can he do it in time?

What if Haarith comes back to check on him? And even if he does manage to reach the street—then what? He already knows what lies ahead if he remains in the cellar: death or humiliation; is he ready for what lies on the outside?

Zayd doesn't know the answer to that. What he does know is that he cannot stay here knowing that his Imam is in danger.

There's only one way to go—forward.

Zayd looks at the wall once again, this time with conviction instead of despair.

Zayd needs your help!

Find the solution to the code and write it in the box below. Then turn to that page number to continue the journey.

If you need some clues, go to page 111

UMAR IBN SA'AD'S TENT

Zayd makes it to the palm trees. He peers around one of them and gasps in shock at the scene before him. What should have been a deserted plain is filled with hundreds, no, thousands...tens of thousands of soldiers! The men are scattered in camps along the Euphrates as far as the eye can see. Hundreds of tents have been pitched. Thousands of horses stand saddled and restlessly stamping their hooves on the hot sand. Men are splashing water on the ground beneath them to keep them cool. The rumble Zayd had heard now becomes the distinct sounds of armed men moving around, shouting orders, sharpening swords, practising strikes; the preparation is underway for an epic battle.

Zayd recognises some of their faces. They are from Kufa. Some of these men had written letters to Imam Husayn inviting him to their city, offering their hospitality and unwavering support. Now they have turned their backs on him and at what price? What have they been threatened with or offered to betray their Imam? Regardless of their motivation, Zayd knows that these men are dangerous; he cannot be discovered.

"Hey, you! Boy!"

Zayd freezes. His eyes dart across the masses to find the source of the voice. A soldier is walking directly towards him. Zayd recognises his face, he is a friend of his uncle.

"Loosen your turban! Uncover your face!"

Zayd panics. He has no choice. The man is surprised to see him.

"What are you doing here, O son of Haarith?"

Time distorts, seconds stretching into eternities. Zayd hates being called Haarith's son. His thoughts become a jumbled maze. The soldier knows who he is, but does he realise that he is here to join Imam Husayn? How should he answer?

"You're soaking wet!" the man continues. "Go and dry off before you touch any of the armour! Don't just stand there like a statue. Go on!"

Zayd cautiously makes his way through the tents. He can feel the eyes of the soldier on his back until he mingles in with the rest of the troops. He is trapped amidst the very enemy he has been trying to avoid! Reason struggles to prevail and Zayd finds himself walking deeper into the camp towards the central tent that is larger than the others. A grotesque man rides up roughly and dismounts his horse with a thud.

He brushes past Zayd, knocking him off balance as he approaches the tent. Zayd notices that he has a scroll clutched in one hand as he folds up the tent flap with the other hand and enters unannounced. Zayd senses that something important is about to happen and that it has to do with the message this man has brought. He cannot linger at the entrance of the tent for long without arousing suspicion. He grabs the man's horse and pretends to tie the reins to the tent post. His knuckles wrap tightly around the coarse leather reins until they turn white.

Zayd leans closer to the tent. He needs to hear the conversation and find out the contents of the letter and who it is from. Raised voices carry out.

"Husayn will never submit..."

"Tell me what you plan to do. Will you carry out what you have been ordered to and engage the enemy?"

Zayd can hear the threat in the second voice. It is a voice that makes him uneasy, it seems laced with evil and malice as it continues, "If you don't, then I have orders for you to hand over the command to me!"

"No, you will not benefit by exploiting this situation," the second man replies. "I will execute Ibn Ziyad's order. You will lead the left flank of the army. We will attack today."

The letter is from Ibn Ziyad with a direct order to attack! Zayd's worst fears are confirmed. Footsteps approach the entrance. He lets go of the reins and quickly staggers away. He turns back to get a glimpse of the men who are leaving. He vaguely recognises the one walking ahead; is it Umar ibn Sa'ad? Even though he has not been openly sympathetic to the Ahlulbayt, Zayd did not expect this from him. Is he being threatened or has he been bribed?

Umar ibn Sa'ad calls out to the nearby soldiers to mount their horses. Are they going to attack now? The midday sun is high above them. Is Zayd too late? Is the battle about to begin while he is stuck on the wrong side?

He watches as the unit detaches itself and gallops to a small group of tents metres away. Emotions collide within his soul as Zayd catches his first sight of Imam Husayn's tents. His heart is overwhelmed with the knowledge that he has reached his goal, but he is terrified by what is about to happen. Tears fill his dark brown eyes.

I am coming, my Imam. I am here!

But how can he cross the enemy lines? He looks at the soldiers around him. Some of their faces reflect his worry. Perhaps they have been forced here, or their conscience is warning them what is happening is wrong. All Zayd knows is that he is not in the right place. He needs to move away from here and fast.

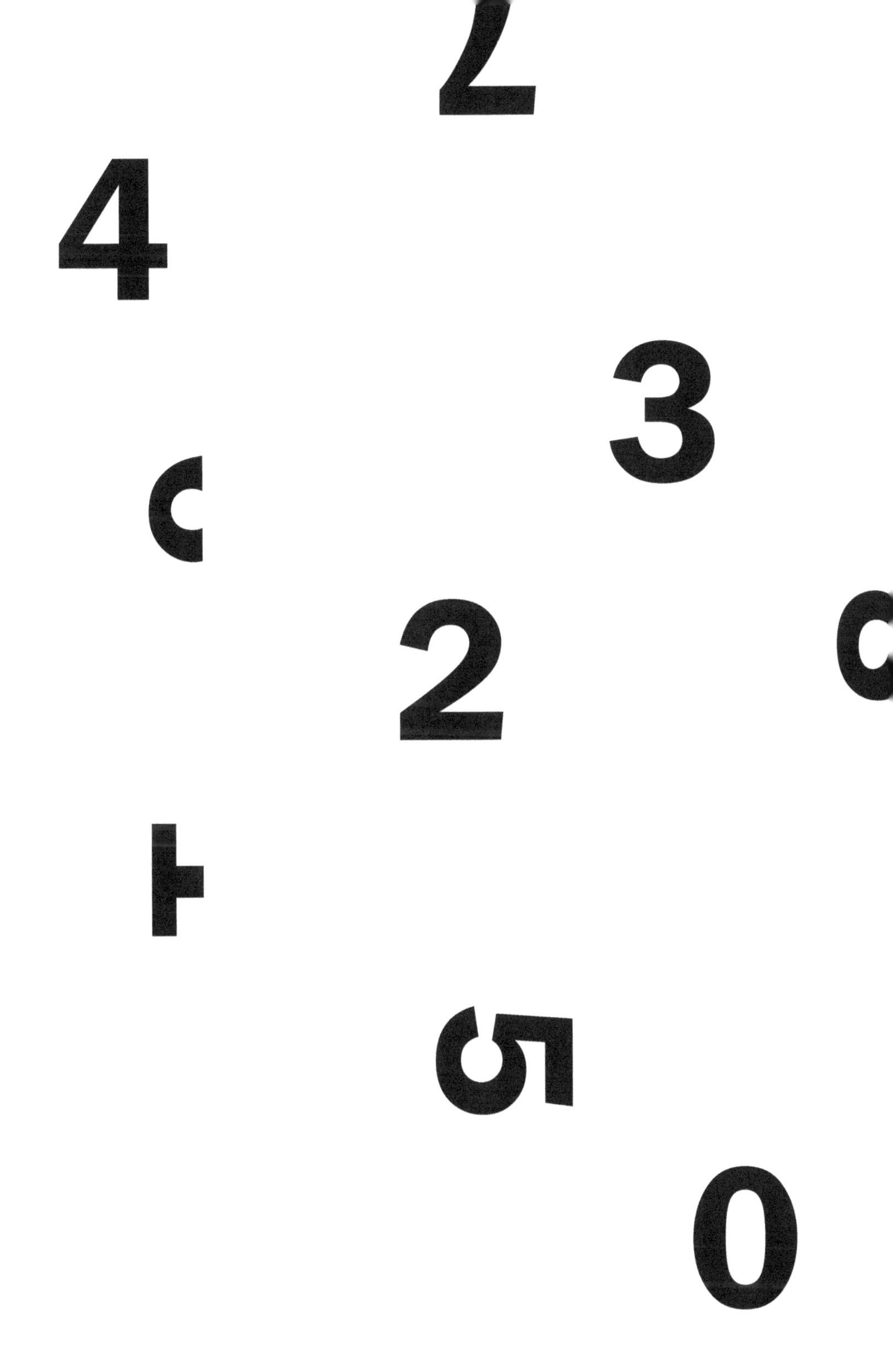

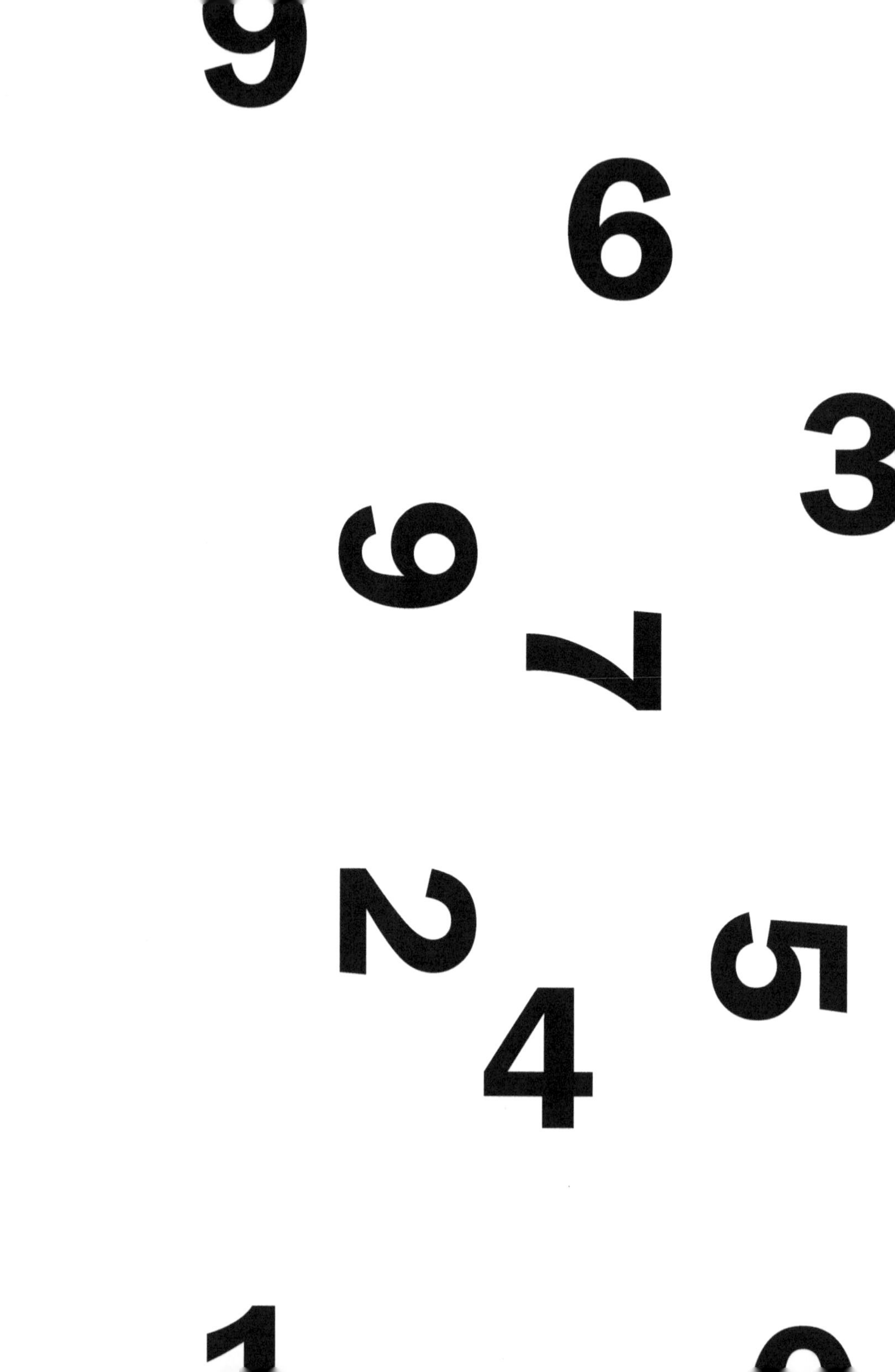

Zayd needs your help!

Find the solution to the code and write it in the box below. Then turn to that page number to continue the journey.

If you need some clues, go to page 113

WAKE UP ZAYD

A sharp pain in Zayd's ankle jolts him awake, it feels as if someone has stabbed his leg. Shock ripples through his nervous system. How long has he been asleep? Did he cut himself on something? He moves his leg and a rustling sound gives away what has happened even before he sees the mottled, writhing ropey creature as it slithers away into the undergrowth. He has been bitten by a snake.

This is the last thing he needs. Zayd groans. He wasn't able to see it well enough to know if the snake was venomous; if it was, he will need to resign himself to imminent death. He carefully lifts his foot. The wound is throbbing already, but it doesn't seem to be worsening yet. Maybe if he was lucky, it might have been a dry bite. He knows a few people who have survived those; not without a great deal of pain, but at least they lived.

He musters up the courage to look at his ankle. Two clear punctures show the site of the wound. There is just a drop of red on each. No flowing blood. That's a good sign.

He pushes himself up on his knees and places one hand on the trunk of the palm tree he was resting against; he tries to stand up. The moment he places his foot on the ground, a sharp, burning sensation travels up his leg. His knees feel like they have turned into runny honey and his legs give way. He moans in pain. Perhaps the bite is worse than he thought.

Zayd has to find water quickly. He is thirsty and needs to clean the wound. He looks at his ankle again—it is visibly swollen and the skin surrounding it is turning a bluish-purple. How will he manage to walk through the forest or even find water? His thoughts turn back to Imam Husayn. How is he managing in the harsh desert? Word is that his family, including women and little children, are with him. They will surely need extra water and provisions. What if they can't find water too? How will the children bear the thirst in the high heat of the scorching desert?

Zayd shakes his head. Catastrophising will not help. He must keep moving and reach where Imam Husayn is camped to see with his own eyes rather than give in to his worst fears. He grabs hold of the tree trunk with both arms using his fingers to get a grip on the ridges in the bark. He tries to stand up again.

Invisible flames of pain lick up his legs and spine and he collapses with a cry of pain against the tree. He pants with effort, his breath coming short and fast. He brings the image of his beloved Imam to his mind and grits his teeth; he must keep moving. Looking around, he searches for a branch he can use for support and finally finds one that is about the right height. He tests it for strength, and it seems able to take his weight. Mustering every ounce of the energy he has remaining, he pulls himself up. The pain shoots up his body, but it is coming in waves. He can work with it and not against it, the trick is to pause when it rises and move when it subsides.

One step at a time. Move the right foot, pause, breathe, drag the left foot forward, pause, breathe, step again...Zayd realises that he is scared, more than he was in the cellar or the tunnel. This is a child-like fear that makes him want to give up and cry. He is not afraid of death, but he does not want to die. Not here, not like this. *Please Allah! Let me live long enough to see my master Husayn... I just want to see him one more time.* Tears of anguish roll down his cheeks, hope and fear mixed in them in equal amounts.

"Do not let pain go to waste," his mother would tell him when he got hurt as a child. "Let it make you stronger." His uncle, Haarith, believed that pain could make a person come to their senses. Zayd doesn't know if he is stronger or more reasonable, all he knows is that he is alive and in agony. Something foreign is travelling through his blood — part venom, part frustration — and it feels like it will poison him slowly, crippling him before he can attain his one desire.

He doesn't know how far he has managed to walk, but he is feeling lightheaded. The world spins and stands still and then it spins again. Zayd pauses. Where is the water? Why is it so far? He just needs to reach it and then he can think straight. He feels dizzy again and lets out a bitter scream of frustration at the betrayal of his own body.

Suddenly a voice fills his head. A familiar voice that he hasn't heard since he was a little boy.

You can do this, Son. Keep going. Do not keep your Imam waiting.

"Father?"

Zayd looks around half expecting to see his father standing in front of him. He calls out again, but only the palm fronds respond with a soft rustling. It must be the poison playing tricks on his mind. Hallucinations are not uncommon after snake bites. The voice had been so clear and Zayd's heart aches. He has missed his father terribly in the past few years. As he makes his journey to manhood, he often wishes that he could turn to his father for advice or answers to the many questions he has about life.

Zayd knows his father would have been proud of what he has achieved tonight. He knows that the words he heard were exactly what his father would have said to him. Zayd will not let his father down. He reaches down and pulls off the sandal from his swollen foot. Releasing it from the restricting straps relieves some of the pressure and eases the pain a little.

Alhamdulillah! He sends a silent prayer of gratitude to the heavens. Looking up for the first time since he escaped the cellar, he realises what a beautiful night it is. The sky is sprinkled with stars. He feels a sense of wonderous awe and hope. The third verse of Surah al-Jaathiya falls from his lips: *"Most surely in the heavens and the earth there are signs for the believers."*

A heady sensation comes over him, he feels faint and his vision blurs...

Zayd needs your help!

Find the solution to the code and write it in the box below. Then turn to that page number to continue the journey.

If you need some clues, go to page 115

SOLDIERS

The darkness of the night is loosening its grip. A sliver of light begins to streak the eastern sky and the world is bathed in a gentle golden glow. Zayd lays flat on the driftwood. He does not want to be seen yet, not even by a traveller or desert dweller. He wants to be able to distinguish between friend and foe before approaching anyone. Truth is mixed with falsehood in every individual around him, except for one: Husayn ibn Ali—he is truth personified. Zayd's heart now beats for Husayn and the closer he reaches, the louder it beats. He is being irresistibly drawn to his destiny.

Zayd pulls himself forward in slow strokes. He peers over the top of the driftwood into the clear waters and considers his reflection. He is pleasantly surprised by his rugged appearance. He looks more grown-up, like a man instead of a young boy. The bruises from his uncle's beating are darkening, but the soft hair on his cheeks look darker and fuller. Zayd feels a sense of pride at his wounds; each one tells the story of his resilience.

A commotion off the banks calls his attention. He quickly moves closer to take a better look at what is happening. A group of soldiers are riding in the distance. They are moving at an urgent pace on horseback; their flags flapping wildly in the wind above their heads. Zayd's realises with horror that they are armed to the teeth. The clang of steel rises above that of the horses' hoofbeats. They are in full armour with swords, shields, axes, and spears strapped to their bodies and beasts. Zayd's mind begins to race. They are riding from the direction of Kufa. Are they soldiers of Ibn Ziyad? Even more men being sent out? Why do they need so many warriors and where are they headed? An uneasy dread fills his entire being.

Zayd decides to follow them. He thrusts himself forward, urgently scooping the water behind him. Ducking down low, he tries to maintain sight of them through the shield of reeds. However, the soldiers are moving too fast, and he soon loses them as they disappear in a cloud of dust. Zayd stops to look at the direction they are travelling in. They seem to be headed towards the land of Taff.

Zayd furrows his brow in confusion. Taff is a barren land with hardly any settlements. Why would an entire army be gathering there? What threat has arisen there that requires such force to eradicate? Worry washes over Zayd. His mind plays out his worst fears. An image of soldiers surrounding Imam Husayn flashes across his mind. Hot, angry tears sting his eyes. Imam Husayn had left Medina to escape these tyrants; he went to Makkah, the sacred city where all creatures of God find peace, and he found himself in such mortal danger that he was forced to leave without completing the Hajj. Now on his way to Kufa, he is facing opposition once again just as his brother before him had.

Zayd imagines how his father would feel to see history repeat itself in such a short space of time. How would he react to the fact that people had deserted their Imam once again? This time is different though. Imam Husayn will not sign a peace treaty. Yazid is not the type of man who would make or uphold any kind of treaty: he is a man who seeks to destroy and annihilate. This is obvious from the strategy Ibn Ziyad has taken in Kufa. Zayd's heart shatters. He knows that Yazid is thirsty for the blood of his beloved Imam and he is so ashamed of his fellow Kufans for their cowardice and disloyalty.

Just moments ago, Zayd had been so proud of his own escape from Kufa. Now he realises that he cannot be happy until he reaches Imam Husayn. There is no news that Imam Husayn has gathered an army of any substance, in fact, he has his family with him! And so many soldiers are heading out on the command of Ibn Ziyad. It does not make sense to Zayd. He cannot afford to stop now. He must track the Euphrates towards Taff and find the camp of Imam Husayn. That is his only home now.

Zayd needs your help!

Find the solution to the code and write it in the box below. Then turn to that page number to continue the journey.

If you need some clues, go to page 117

INSIDE THE TUNNEL

Bismillahir Rahmaanir Raheem. Zayd moves the handle to the correct position. The metal bar of the gate slides open in a surprisingly smooth motion and the gate swings open silently. A stale, musty scent rises up from the belly of the tunnel. It smells of darkness. A darkness that awaits him. He steps in cautiously and is hit with the wall of silence. It is as if he has left Kufa behind in another world. The childhood tales of the jinn that live in these tunnels come rushing back to him. He places one foot in front of another on the soft, damp ground, and the muffled echo of his footsteps seem to mingle with whispers that just escape his hearing.

A sudden **BANG** makes him jump and his heart leaps to his throat. Spinning around to face the source of the sound, he realises that the darkness is as solid behind him as it is ahead. The gate has slammed shut, but there was no draft or wind to cause such a violent movement of the heavy door. Was it the hand of a jinn that had pushed it? Is he trapped by a creature of the unseen now, an easy prey to its appetite? All of Zayd's senses are activated and on high alert.

Now shut in the tunnel he chose to enter; he turns back and tries to maintain his orientation. He continues to walk into the unknown darkness ahead of him, his outstretched hand grazing the rough walls as he traverses the meandering path. The stone beneath his fingers is textured with tales of forgotten history, etched into the rock like a code waiting to be deciphered. As he walks, he begins to sense small changes in his surroundings. The soft earth has given way to small pebbles that now crunch beneath his feet.

The air is thicker, harder to breath cleanly. It reminds him of the grave. He glances over his shoulder as if he can see, but all is still dark and shadowed. Whatever dangers lie around him, they are concealed and can pounce without notice. He is helpless and paranoia reaches out its claws to cripple his heart.

A distant voice pierces the silence. It is soft and melodious. Not at all what Zayd expects to hear. The fear releases its hold, reluctantly at first, but then as he recognises the words and melody of the Quran, it dissipates completely.

Whoever is reciting…is not a jinn. The voice is filtering down from one of the houses above him. He sighs with relief. Stopping for a break, he leans against the tunnel wall and strains to make out the exact verse.

"Only Allah is your Wali and His Messenger and those who believe, those who keep up prayers and pay the poor rate while they bow."

Five, fifty-five. Long-forgotten memories come flooding back. Zayd's grandfather had met the Holy Prophet, and he would tell the best stories about the Prophet's character and his mannerisms with people. One of Zayd's favourite stories had been the one about a poor man who had entered the masjid looking for charity. When Imam Ali stretched out his finger to give the poor man his ring whilst in the state of rukuh, this verse had been revealed.

Only Allah is your Wali and His Messenger and those who believe...

Sadly, during the time of the second caliph, the transmission of the sunnah had been banned. Zayd knows that this is why although many Kufans, including his uncle, have memorised the Quran and recite it beautifully, they remain unfamiliar with how these verses relate to the Household of the Prophet and what their inextricable connection to the Holy Book is. Haarith, like most of his peers, only attaches himself to the Ahlulbayt when it suits his interest or when instructed to by their tribal leader.

Hearing these verses echoing in the dredges of the foundations of Kufa on the same night that people are turning their backs on the family of the Prophet saddens Zayd more than he can bear. He has known that Imam Husayn's life was in danger from the moment he heard that the Imam had secretly left Medina after his confrontation with Walid, the governor of Medina. Yazid is stubborn and when he wants something he will do anything to get it. How far is he willing to go for the pledge of allegiance from Imam Husayn? Zayd wonders at his own naivety in thinking that the Kufans would have a conscience and stay loyal to the invitation they had sent Imam Husayn. Zayd has lived amongst these people and has witnessed their fickle nature firsthand. He should have known better.

Zayd isn't looking to be a hero, but he knows that if he lets anything happen to the grandson of the Holy Prophet without doing something—anything—he would never be able to hold his head high with any sense of self-respect. That is why he is here, in the heart of a tomb-like tunnel, covered in mud, dust and blood, counting the minutes to sunrise and seeking out his fate, whether it be death by the side of his Imam or on his way to him.

He does not know where the tunnel will lead, but he cannot go back. Exhaustion is catching up with him and he can feel the weight of his own body. His steps are growing heavier; soon he is shuffling forward rather than walking. Suddenly, the passage narrows in. He can feel the walls close on either side until he is almost moving sideways in the tunnel's embrace.

He gasps as his hand and then shoulder come to the end of the path. It is a solid wall of stone. The end of the tunnel is blocked by what feels like huge boulders. He screams out in despair, scrabbling at the rocks. Is this to be his end after already escaping one underground prison? To be buried alive in another of his own choosing?

No!

The face of Imam Husayn flashes in front of his eyes. Zayd's heart is filled with love at the beautiful visage, that sweet, gentle smile filled with love and mercy.

No! It cannot be over.

He has made an intention to reach his Imam and he will make it or die trying until the last second of his life.

With a determination he had not thought himself capable of, Zayd shakes his head, clearing his mind. He begins to run his hands along the boulders. These boulders have either fallen or been placed here. There must be a weak spot somewhere. Perhaps he can find a loose piece to dislodge?

0	0	0	0	0	0	0	0	0	0	0	0	0	0	0	0	0	0	0	0	0	0	0	0	0	0	0	0	0	0	0	0	0	0
0	0	0	0	0	0	0	0	0	0	0	0	0	0	0	0	0	0	0	0	0	0	0	0	0	0	0	0	0	0	0	0	0	0
0	0	0	0	0	0	0	0	0	0	0	0	0	0	0	0	0	0	0	0	0	0	0	0	0	0	0	0	0	0	0	0	0	0
0	0	0	0	0	0	0	0	0	0	0	0	0	0	0	0	0	0	0	0	0	0	0	0	0	0	0	0	0	0	0	0	0	0
0	0	0	0	0	0	0	0	0	0	0	0	0	0	0	0	0	0	0	0	0	0	0	0	0	0	0	0	0	0	0	0	0	0
0	0	0	0	0	0	0	0	0	0	0	0	0	0	0	0	0	0	0	0	0	0	0	0	0	0	0	0	0	0	0	0	0	0
0	0	0	0	0	0	0	0	0	0	0	0	0	0	0	0	0	0	0	0	0	0	0	0	0	0	0	0	0	0	0	0	0	0
0	0	0	0	0	0	0	0	0	0	0	0	0	0	0	0	0	0	0	0	0	0	0	0	0	0	0	0	0	0	0	0	0	0
0	0	0	0	0	0	0	0	0	0	0	0	0	0	0	0	0	0	0	0	0	0	0	0	0	0	0	0	0	0	0	0	0	0
0	0	0	0	0	0	0	0	0	0	0	0	0	0	0	0	0	0	0	0	0	0	0	0	0	0	0	0	0	0	0	0	0	0
0	0	0	0	0	0	0	0	0	0	0	0	0	0	0	0	0	0	0	0	0	0	0	0	0	0	0	0	0	0	0	0	0	0
0	0	0	0	0	0	0	0	0	0	0	0	0	0	0	0	0	0	0	0	0	0	0	0	0	0	0	0	0	0	0	0	0	0
0	0	0	0	0	0	0	0	0	0	0	0	0	0	0	0	0	0	0	0	0	0	0	0	0	0	0	0	0	0	0	0	0	0
0	0	0	0	0	0	0	0	0	0	0	0	0	0	0	0	0	0	0	0	0	0	0	0	0	0	0	0	0	0	0	0	0	0
0	0	0	7	0	0	0	0	0	0	0	0	0	0	0	7	0	0	0	0	0	0	0	0	0	0	0	0	0	0	0	0	0	0
0	0	0	0	0	0	0	0	0	0	0	0	0	0	0	0	0	0	0	0	0	0	0	0	0	0	0	0	0	0	0	0	0	0
0	0	0	0	0	0	0	0	0	0	0	0	0	0	0	0	0	0	0	0	0	0	0	0	0	0	0	0	0	0	0	0	0	0
0	0	0	0	0	0	0	0	0	0	0	0	0	0	0	0	0	0	0	0	0	0	0	0	0	0	0	0	0	0	0	0	0	0
0	0	0	0	0	0	0	0	0	0	0	0	0	0	0	0	0	0	0	0	0	0	0	0	0	0	0	0	0	0	0	0	0	0

0	0	0	0	0	0	0	0	0	0	0	0	0	0	0	0	0	0	0	0	0	0	0	0	0	0	0	0	0	0	0	0	0	0	0	0	0	0	0	0	0
0	0	0	0	0	0	0	0	0	0	0	0	0	0	0	0	0	0	0	0	0	0	0	0	0	0	0	0	0	0	0	0	0	0	0	0	0	7	0	0	0
0	0	0	0	0	0	0	0	0	0	0	0	0	0	0	0	0	0	0	0	0	0	0	0	0	0	0	0	0	0	0	0	0	0	0	0	0	0	0	0	0
0	0	0	0	0	0	0	0	0	0	0	0	0	0	0	0	0	0	0	0	0	0	0	0	0	0	0	0	0	0	0	0	0	0	0	0	0	0	0	0	0
0	0	0	0	0	0	0	0	0	0	0	0	0	0	0	0	0	0	0	0	0	0	0	0	0	0	0	0	0	0	0	0	0	0	0	0	0	0	0	0	0
0	0	0	0	0	0	0	0	0	0	0	0	0	0	0	0	0	0	0	0	0	0	0	0	0	0	0	0	0	0	0	0	0	0	0	0	0	0	0	0	0
0	0	0	0	0	0	0	0	0	0	0	0	0	0	0	0	0	0	0	0	0	0	0	0	0	0	0	0	0	0	0	0	0	0	0	0	0	0	0	0	0
0	0	0	0	0	0	0	0	0	0	0	0	0	0	0	0	0	0	0	0	0	0	0	0	0	0	0	0	0	0	0	0	0	0	0	0	0	0	0	0	0
0	0	0	0	0	0	0	0	0	0	0	0	0	0	0	0	0	0	0	0	0	0	0	0	0	0	0	0	0	0	0	0	0	0	0	0	0	0	0	0	0
0	0	0	0	0	0	0	0	0	0	0	0	0	0	0	0	0	0	0	0	0	0	0	0	0	0	0	0	0	0	0	0	0	0	0	0	0	0	0	0	0
0	0	0	0	0	0	0	0	0	0	0	0	0	0	0	0	0	0	0	0	0	0	0	0	0	0	0	0	0	0	0	0	0	0	0	0	0	0	0	0	0
0	0	0	0	0	0	0	0	0	0	0	0	0	0	0	0	0	0	0	0	0	0	0	0	0	0	0	0	0	0	0	0	0	0	0	0	0	0	0	0	0
0	0	0	0	0	0	0	0	0	0	0	0	0	0	0	0	0	0	0	0	0	0	0	0	0	0	0	0	0	0	0	0	0	0	0	0	0	0	0	0	0
0	0	0	0	0	0	0	0	0	0	0	0	0	0	0	0	0	0	0	0	0	0	0	0	0	0	0	0	0	0	0	0	0	0	0	0	0	0	0	0	0
0	0	0	0	0	0	0	0	0	0	0	0	0	0	0	0	0	0	0	0	0	0	0	0	0	0	0	0	0	0	0	0	0	0	0	0	0	0	0	0	0
0	0	0	0	0	0	0	0	0	0	0	0	0	0	0	0	0	0	0	0	0	0	0	0	0	0	0	0	0	0	0	0	0	0	0	0	0	0	0	0	0
0	0	0	0	0	0	0	0	0	0	0	0	0	0	0	0	0	0	0	0	0	0	0	0	0	0	0	0	0	0	0	0	0	0	0	0	0	0	0	0	0
0	0	0	0	0	0	0	0	0	0	0	0	0	0	0	0	0	0	0	0	0	0	0	0	0	0	0	0	0	0	0	0	0	0	0	0	0	0	0	0	0
0	0	0	0	0	0	0	0	0	0	0	0	0	0	0	0	0	0	0	0	0	0	0	0	0	0	0	0	0	0	0	0	0	0	0	0	0	0	0	0	0
0	0	0	0	0	0	0	0	0	0	0	0	0	0	0	0	0	0	0	0	0	0	0	0	0	0	0	0	0	0	0	0	0	0	0	0	0	0	0	0	0

Zayd needs your help!

Find the solution to the code and write it in the box below. Then turn to that page number to continue the journey.

If you need some clues, go to page 119

THE MOTHER BIRD

Zayd has been wandering for a while now. His vision fades and clears; his senses seem suspended in that dream-like space between consciousness and unconsciousness, but he keeps moving. Sometimes he leans against a tree to catch his breath and breathe through the pain. It has become a companion now, washing over him almost hesitantly as if reluctant to bring him so much grief. When the pain is manageable, he pushes through the trees again, seeking out the water he so desperately needs. He has walked for so long; it feels like he should have reached the Euphrates by now! Is he going the right way? Or has he been walking in fruitless circles?

Sweat continually drips down his temples. Nausea overcomes him and Zayd gags. His body shudders from the convulsions rising up from his belly, but there is nothing in it to bring up. Zayd had argued with Haarith before they had a chance to begin the evening meal.

He shivers and wills himself to take another step. He turns to the right and then to the left, searching for any indication or sign of direction. His breathing is ragged and strained.

Is this what poison does to a human body? This state of living hell, where death seems like it would be a welcome release? Zayd's mind goes back to the last days of Imam Hasan and how the poison had affected his body. Those gathered around him could not bear to look upon his face. Once shining and fair, it had now turned as yellow and pale as the medicated cloth that was bound around his forehead to ease his suffering.

Although it was not the first time Imam Hasan had been poisoned, this final time had been with a specially concocted poison of the deadliest variety. Muawiya had bribed Imam Hasan's own wife to administer it. Zayd wondered how these repeated betrayals from those closest to him had hurt the Imam, who had given nothing but love and kindness to all. How he must have suffered, both emotionally and physically!

Zayd recounts the scene like a movie in his mind: Imam Husayn sitting beside his brother's bed, watching him cough up blood, holding his hand, weeping and yet trying to comfort him. He remembers the strange statement Imam Hasan had made in response to his younger brother's sympathy.

What had he meant? No one has been able to figure out what these words signify. Zayd wonders what could be more calamitous than poison squeezing out your life from within your body. What could be worse than a lifetime of betrayal and treachery? What is the day of Husayn going to be? The urgency of this question pushes Zayd forward. He looks around desperately for a clue or a sign.

A sudden, swift movement in the air catches his attention. A small, feathered creature lands lightly on a branch near his head. A bird! At this time of the night? She looks at him and tilts her head questioningly as if to ask, "What are you doing out?" He is fascinated by this little bird who doesn't emit a sound but continues to hold his gaze. Zayd doesn't dare to inhale in case he scares her away. He can't understand what a lone bird is doing out in the dark; the snake that bit him could make an easy meal out of her in one mouthful. The night is the domain of the predator after all.

Are you running away too? Zayd wonders silently. She looks indignantly at him and hops away to the next branch. He soon realises that she has a very different purpose. He watches as she hops over a leaf, climbs carefully up a twig, and then jumps over a flower to reach a tucked-away nest filled with tiny open mouths. She is a mother and was carrying water in her beak for her chicks! Zayd watches as she drops the precious liquid into each mouth, making sure every baby gets its due. Once she is done, she finally chirps—a comforting farewell to her little ones— and then flies away. She stops on a branch high up ahead and chirps again. Well? Are you coming? she seems to be asking and then she is gone. Zayd watches her disappear between the trees. Has she gone to get more water? Then it must be close by!

Mesmerised by the encounter, Zayd realises that the courage of the mother bird in facing the dangers of the night comes from the love she has for her young ones. Love gives her courage. Love will give him courage too. *I am no longer running away from anyone,* Zayd thinks to himself as he follows the direction the bird flew in. I am now running towards my beloved.

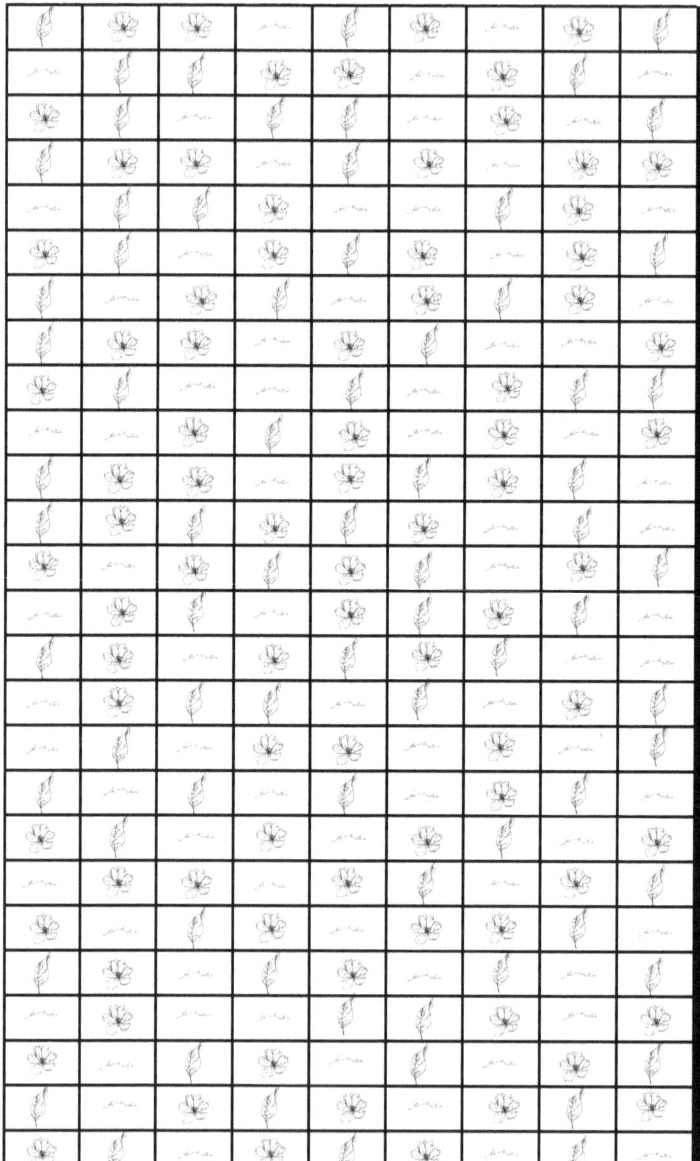

7
4
A
6
2
P
3
4
5
9
M
8
4
L
0
7
H
8
1
4
3
0
Y
5
Z
4

Zayd needs your help!

Find the solution to the code and write it in the box below. Then turn to that page number to continue the journey.

If you need some clues, go to page 121

THE ENEMY CAMP

The midday sun burns down on Zayd's back. He can feel its prickly heat through his shirt. His tattered turban affords some covering for his head, he has loosened it so that he can shield his face from the merciless glare. As he peers out from under it, he notices men further ahead along the riverbank. Soldiers again! Zayd quickly covers his face and pulls himself to the shore. Why are there soldiers patrolling the river? He quickly makes the decision to let the driftwood float away downstream. It served him well, but he can no longer continue along the water. His journey will have to be on foot once again.

Keeping his face covered, he hides amongst the reeds and continues to spy on the men, trying to gather clues. Zayd can now hear horses and a steady rumbling in the distance. The soldiers he can see don't seem to be collecting any water, they are simply guarding the area. He can't make any sense of it. Arab etiquette dictates that the river belongs to everyone and no one should ever be denied water, so who are they keeping away from it?

The only time Zayd has ever heard of soldiers cutting off a water supply is in the story of the Battle of Siffin. His mother narrated the story to him as she had heard it from his father. Muawiya's army took control of the water supply and denied access to Imam Ali's army. The thirsty men had to fight to reach it and with the Grace of God, they managed to do so. When Imam Ali's army gained control of the water, they petitioned him to treat the enemy in the same manner. But Ali bin Abi Talib was not like Muawiyah, Zayd's mother had told him with pride in her voice. Free access to the water was given to all: friend and foe alike.

Zayd gets a sinking feeling in the pit of his stomach at this recollection. Yazid is the son of Muawiya and in many ways worse than his father. He will have no qualms about leaving those he considers his enemy thirsty and at this moment in time, his enemy is Husayn son of Ali.

Zayd feels as if he has had all the air sucked out of his lungs. The apprehension is worse than anything he has had to bear so far. His uncle's torture, the choking tunnels, the agony of the poison—he would go through all of those over and over again rather than consider the possibility that Imam Husayn and his family—his children!—were possibly thirsty in the scorching heat of the desert with no clear access to water.

That can't be true, he tells himself, these are human beings, surely they would not do such a thing! Hot tears flow from Zayd's eyes. He swallows hard, but he feels as if his throat is filled with brambles and he chokes. He cannot afford to give in to panic. He reminds himself to breathe. In and out... in and out.

Crouching between the reeds and palm trees, Zayd knows he must find a path through them. Imam Husayn must be nearby and his sole purpose of existence now is to reach him.

A	F	A	F	J	K	R	A	Y	T	L	O	C	K
S	O	R	B	W	J	K	L	C	E	Q	V	B	N
Q	L	P	G	B	H	Y	U	C	N	S	U	Z	L
P	L	U	I	L	A	X	G	S	T	K	L	D	E
O	O	X	B	N	M	S	A	J	K	R	A	Y	Y
M	W	J	D	Z	A	I	N	A	B	H	P	M	A
N	T	H	E	P	L	N	B	I	S	M	I	H	I
D	W	A	T	A	R	H	Y	S	A	U	N	K	A
R	B	A	L	T	H	A	N	O	T	T	H	I	S
L	E	T	T	E	T	R	U	M	A	R	I	B	N
S	K	A	A	B	O	W	A	Y	T	D	O	N	T
R	A	T	H	I	T	H	E	C	E	K	T	H	A
U	R	U	B	A	Y	D	A	O	N	L	L	A	H
N	B	I	B	N	Z	I	Y	D	T	A	D	S	T
B	A	Y	O	U	C	A	N	E	O	G	E	A	H
R	L	D	Y	A	M	F	O	F	N	T	W	H	E
E	A	Q	U	E	U	E	A	Y	E	S	E	M	E
A	E	T	H	S	O	U	W	T	H	O	V	U	N
K	V	W	E	C	A	N	A	D	E	V	E	N	R
S	E	O	D	A	L	D	T	B	A	M	L	L	O
N	N	N	O	P	I	W	E	I	S	N	A	O	T
A	M	F	M	E	M	Y	R	G	O	O	D	E	F
K	A	V	O	U	R	I	S	A	N	D	T	V	E
E	P	M	U	H	A	R	R	A	M	D	A	I	Y
R	T	A	F	F	M	O	T	R	U	T	H	L	Q
D	F	G	H	A	L	P	U	N	M	W	E	R	Y

Zayd needs your help!

Find the solution to the code and write it in the box below. Then turn to that page number to continue the journey.

If you need some clues, go to page 123

ACCESSING THE TUNNEL

Zayd looks at the sky. The dark plum of the midnight sky is starting to lighten ever so slightly. Sunrise is approaching and Zayd has not reached the gate yet. He is close. He knows it must be just a street down, but navigating around the guards has been a formidable challenge. He has had to crouch in corners and stay still for endless minutes only to be able to move a few steps before another guard approaches and forces him to hide again. They seem to be everywhere like swarming ants.

If he doesn't make it to the tunnels soon, the light will give him away and all his efforts will be in vain. The guards will find him and take him to Ibn Ziyad who will probably hand him back to his uncle.

Haarith! Zayd breathes a sharp intake of the cold night air. What if his uncle comes back to check on him? What will he do when he realises that Zayd is gone? The footholds and the hole in the cellar wall will be clear indicators of his route to freedom. Haarith will be enraged, no doubt, but what will he do with that anger? Will he come after Zayd or… Zayd's thoughts turn to the one other person Haarith could target: his beloved mother.

She has been left behind yet again. Zayd tries to imagine the look on her face when she realises that he has gone. Will Haarith tell her why he ran away? Of course he will. Ibn Ziyad has sworn to punish entire tribes if a single person is found to have disobeyed. Haarith will take every opportunity to lay the blame for any consequences on Zayd and Zayd alone.

Tears well up in Zayd's eyes as he remembers the soft embrace of his mother. How he longs for the comfort of her arms and the stroke of her hand on his hair. Even though he was only a child, he remembers how she had reacted when news of his father's murder reached Kufa. Her knees gave way and she fell to the ground. At first, people called for water, thinking she has fainted, but then they realised she was actually prostrating in gratitude, thanking God for the honour of being married to a man who had remained loyal to the Ahlulbayt till his last breath. His father's bravery was in part due to his mother's support.

Yes, his mother would hold him and comfort him if she was with him, but then she would whisper words of encouragement and send him onwards in service to his Imam.

Be proud of me, Mother. Pray for my success.

***

One of Zayd's earliest and most vivid memories is from the year when his mother took him to Makkah to perform the Hajj for the first time. He remembers the feel of his mother's ihram between his fingers as he clung to the coarse white cloth. They began to slowly circumambulate the House of God together. She recited the takbeer and he repeated it after her. They were almost at the corner where the Black Stone is housed in its niche when a commotion arose. A small crowd of people were walking towards the Ka'ba, and it seemed as if they were surrounding a precious, important entity. Shouts of *Allahu Akbar!* and *La ilaaha illalah!* rose in the air as they neared the Holy House.

Suddenly, the crowd parted—in the way the seas must have for Musa—and a stunning man walked out from its midst. He approached the Black Stone, walking in the direction where Zayd and his mother stood. Zayd's mother brought him forward so he could see the man clearly; he had plentiful curly hair that framed a smooth luminescent face. His graceful neck was as white as jug of silver, and he walked humbly on the earth.

Zayd felt drawn to the man and something deep within him stirred. As if in response to this feeling, he looked down sympathetically at Zayd with what seemed to be tears glistening in his eyes. He cupped Zayd's chin in his hand and leaned down to whisper glad tidings of paradise for his father along with a prayer for Zayd's faith and attachment to the Ahlulbayt. Zayd can still feel the warm, perfumed breath on his cheek and the sincerity of the prayer that has accompanied him throughout his life. The love, hope and appreciation, the energy of that moment, still runs through his veins.

Imam Hasan is most like the Messenger of Allah, in form, manner and nobility. Zayd can attest to the truth of these words with all his heart and soul.

***

"Calm down Zayd," he says to himself. "You have the prayer of Imam Hasan and the prayers of your mother. You cannot fail!" He concentrates on the present. What can he do here and now? Mustering all his courage and strength, Zayd makes the dash across the last street. He almost cries in relief when he spots the old, rusting gateway that he has been seeking for so long.

He collapses against the iron gate and pauses only to take a few deep breaths before yanking on the handle. He tries once, twice…it doesn't budge. He pulls at it again, frantically now, but nothing moves. It's locked! Tears choke him, he bites his lip and opens the wound on it again. The taste of blood—sharp and salty—brings him back to his senses. He stops to think. The memory of Imam Hasan at the Ka'ba rushes through him. The lashes for disobedience sting his back. He has been through so much; he cannot stop now.

His father's martyrdom, his mother's sacrifices, everything has been leading to this moment. He cannot stand by and let anything terrible happen to Imam Husayn and his family. How could he look the Prophet or Imam Ali in the eye knowing that he did not do everything possible to help their son?

Remembering his goal gives Zayd energy and focus. He steps back and takes a long look at the gate. He notices a wooden plaque nailed above it. It is covered in dust and crumbling in some places. He reaches up and uses the cuff of his sleeve to wipe away the sand. There are letters inscribed on the wooden surface spelling out a message.

SEMITEERHTELDNAHEHTNRUTEDOCEHTDNIFOT

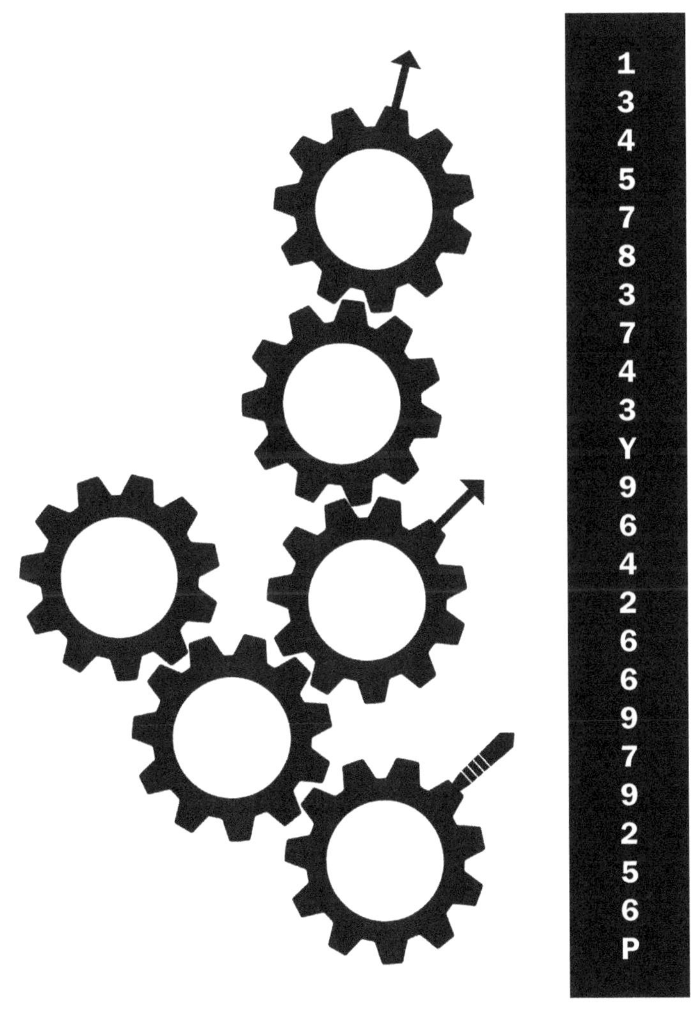

Zayd needs your help!

Find the solution to the code and write it in the box below. Then turn to that page number to continue the journey.

If you need some clues, go to page 125

REACHING IMAM HUSAYN

Zayd watches as Umar ibn Sa'ad and his group of soldiers stop at a distance from Imam Husayn's camp. There is a shout as the commander calls out. After a short wait, there is some movement from the Imam's camp. A handful of horses ride out, their hooves striking the arid earth with muffled thumps.

When they meet, the men descend from their horses and start to talk. One figure stands head and shoulders above the others. The Hashimite men stand at a respectful distance behind him, and the enemies step back warily. The strength of his presence is palpable. A warmth blossoms within Zayd as he recognizes the one they call the Qamar – the full, shining moon – of the Bani Hashim; it is Abul Fadhl Abbas. His tall muscular frame and noble stature cannot be mistaken.

Zayd cannot hear their conversation, but he can no longer wait. The energy coursing through his body compels him to move. He needs to cross from this hell into the heaven that is just beyond his reach. Everyone is concentrating on the exchange between the two groups ahead. This is his only opportunity, there is no looking back.

Fixing his eyes on Abul Fadhl, he begins to dart across the open desert. The world falls into a silence where the only sound is the wind whistling past his ears. Zayd thinks he might make it without anyone noticing. Then he hears the shouts as the surrounding soldiers realise he is breaking the ranks.

"Hey! Where are you going?"

"What do you think you are doing, boy?"

"Come back!"

The voices are loud behind him, but Zayd does not dare to look back .

He hears the rhythmic pounding of boots behind him. Someone is following him! He throws a quick glance behind and sees the soldier who had recognised him earlier closing in on him. He cannot be caught by this man! He propels himself forward with every reserve he has left. The soldier is bigger and stronger, but Zayd is faster and more energetic. Zayd can hear him grunting as he struggles to keep up.

"Come here, you traitor!" the man yells and Zayd feels a hand grabbing at his shirt. He cries out aloud in frustration, he cannot…will not…be stopped. Leaning forward, he pulls against the grasp and his worn shirt tears easily. Zayd stumbles and scrambles away, kicking up dust and sand.

"You stupid boy! You will be killed! I will make sure of it!"

The words of the soldier carry to him as he closes the final few metres, but he does not care for his own life anymore. Imam Husayn's tents are getting closer. He can sense the peace emanating from them. He can smell the heavenly scent carrying out into the desert. A million thoughts rush through Zayd's mind, but above them all, he repeats one name like a litany.

Husayn.

Husayn.

Husayn.

His feet sink into the sand and his pace slows down. He is stumble-running now, clumsy and desperate. He can see Abul Fadhl Abbas returning from the tents to speak with Umar ibn Sa'ad's people. No one sees him because they are all looking at Abbas.

Zayd avoids the group and runs past them at a distance. He collapses face down near the outer tents. Battered and bruised, he lays his sunburnt cheek on the scorching desert sand; his muscles slacken, limbs grow weak. Has he finally made it?

"My Imam," the whisper escapes his lips. "I am here."

Zayd can feel his conscious ebb and flow. He has nothing left in him. He sighs. Suddenly, strong arms lift him up and turn him over. A gentle hand brushes away the dust from his face and smooths back his hair. Zayd basks in the love and safety of the embrace, feeling for a moment as if he is in his mother's arms once again. He opens his eyes and sees the radiant face of Imam Husayn looking down upon him with concern.

Zayd begins to cry. The tears flow uncontrolably, and he is choking on his sobs, but he cannot stop. He has made it and he is with his Imam. Zayd struggles to get on all fours, trying to stand. Imam Husayn helps him pick himself up from the ground. Zayd inhales deeply, the perfumed scent of the Imam filling his senses. He tries to stand up straighter, to show his purpose. "My Master," he says, "I have come to join you. Please accept me."

Imam Husayn smiles, nods and then envelops Zayd in a tight embrace. Zayd allows himself to drown in the strength, the wisdom, the security, the all-encompassing love of that hug. A tidal wave of emotions overcomes him and he faints in the arms of his Master.

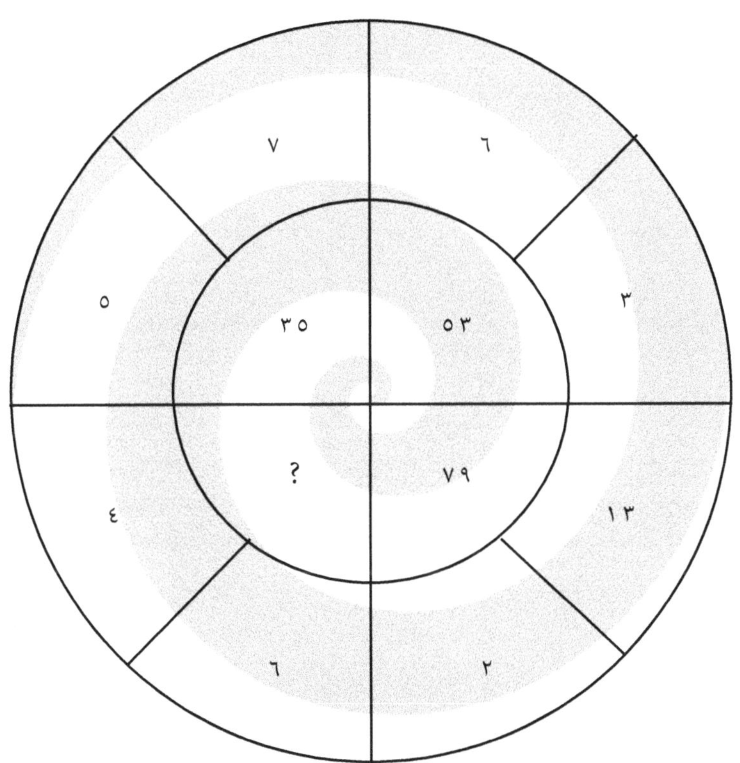

Zayd needs your help!

Find the solution to the code and write it in the box below. Then turn to that page number to continue the journey.

If you need some clues, go to page 127

THE STREETS OF KUFA

Zayd squeezes his slim frame through the gap between the wall and the street. He sends up silent thanks to Allah for the narrow build that he has often been teased about throughout his youth. It has saved precious minutes in the time he spent widening the hole that was his escape route. Although he has smears of mud drying on his arms and his shirt is torn in a few places, he has not hurt himself while scraping through the narrow space. Adrenaline pulses through him and temporarily numbs the soreness from his uncle's thrashing. He looks up at the clear night sky, the moon is still high up which means he has a few hours before sunrise. He needs to be out of Kufa before then. Umayyid guards are patrolling the streets throughout the night curfew, searching for any sign of dissonance to crack down on.

No sooner does he think of them than the sound of footsteps approach accompanied by the distinct *chink* of metal. Guards! Zayd holds his breath and presses his back against the wall, trying to blend into it as much as possible. The men march and turn the corner into the alley before his hiding place. He releases his breath, the whisper of tasbeeh constant under his breath. Thank you, Allah; Please, Allah. Thank you for bringing me this far; Please let me make it to my Imam. Zayd's legs are trembling and his breath is shallow, the air suffocating him as he inhales. It feels like his body will betray him and give up, but he has no choice. He cannot die hiding like this in the dark alleys of Kufa. This is not what his father would have wanted; this is not what *he* wants.

Make a plan.

That is what he needs. A sense of direction and steps to follow. He already knows he must escape Kufa. What he doesn't know is how to do it. The city gates are locked, and no one is allowed to leave without express permission from Ibn Ziyad himself. There is no way out through the streets; there is no way to make it over the city walls either. Zayd sighs. If only he could burrow under the wall like a desert fox....

Suddenly he straightens up as if struck by lightning. Underground! Of course! He should have thought of that! There are old tunnel networks all over the city. Zayd remembers playing near them as a child. He never dared to enter them after hearing all the stories about the jinn who lives in the tunnel looking for young boys to eat. He knows the stories are not true. Just tales to keep the kids away, but he has never ventured near the neglected gateway even after becoming a teenager.

He remembers the closest entry to them. It is a couple of alleys from here and tucked away into a niche between two houses.

The tunnel entrance is not far from the city gates and Zayd is pretty sure it leads to the edge of town. Right now, it is his best—and only—option and he'll still need to cross some streets to get there. He begins to move, the first sense of taking action, of doing something towards his goal, gives him renewed energy. He creeps along the walls of the quiet houses and silent courtyards. Many of the Kufan men have left with the commanders that Ibn Ziyad has been sending out over the past few days. Those who remain are sleeping peacefully with their families.

Zayd wonders at their indifference. How can they rest in their beds while Husayn ibn Ali wanders the hostile desert? He remembers the stories his mother told him of Imam Ali and Imam Hasan walking these same streets at night taking care of the orphans and widows. When she spoke about them, her eyes would light up and her voice would soften. She was drawn to the Ahlulbayt like a moth to a flame. They entranced her and she could talk about their angelic qualities for hours. Zayd has spent his childhood years watching her animated face and listening to her words, the love she held for the blessed family overflowing from her heart and into his.

It still puzzles Zayd; this open hypocrisy and apathy. How can so much change so quickly? How can the hearts of people turn so completely? Kufa is a town full of paradoxes and inconsistencies. The fiercest warriors become spineless cowards. The memorisers of the Quran are the ones who turn against the Ahlulbayt. They pledge their allegiances and write letters of invitation, yet they have no understanding of what the word loyalty means. Zayd knows well what this word means and what it demands of a person. This is the last lesson his father left for him and he holds it close to his heart.

***

"Tell me about my father," Zayd would beg whenever his heart yearned for the man he could barely remember.

His mother would smile at his earnest question. Although widowed at a young age and left with a three-year-old in tow to support, his mother held the few years she had spent with his father in precious memory. She had loved her husband and was fiercely proud of the man he had been. She would recount to Zayd the story of how Imam Hasan became the successor to Imam Ali; how Zayd's father had fallen in love with Imam Hasan's gentleness and kindness with the same passion he had for Imam Ali's bravery and principles.

Zayd's father had joined the majority of Kufa in pledging his support and rallying behind Imam Hasan. Kufa had armed itself and got ready to fight off the attack from Muawiya. Zayd's father had been filled with hope at the prospect of fighting alongside his Imam for truth until the betrayal happened...

Zayd's mother's face would darken, her brow furrowing and her eyes watering whenever she reached this part of the story. The insidious rumours crept in slowly at first and when the bribes followed, their poison spread quickly throughout the army of Imam Hasan. His followers began to leave him one by one, and before long the army had disintegrated and dispersed to the wind like grains of sand in a storm. Even some of those who had seemed to be the closest companions of the Imam were seduced by money or persuaded to keep silent for fear of death.

"Aaah, this dunya," his mother would say, with a heart-wrenching sigh. "Beware of this dunya, Habibi Zayd. It is nothing but a deceiver." She would run her hand over his head, and he would hold his breath for her next words, mouthing them silently with her. "But not for your father. Alhamdulillah, he was not deceived by it." Her voice would swell with pride as she related the rest of the story.

Zayd's father had rushed to Imam Hasan's tent after the mutiny had become apparent. He found the group of close companions in chaos. The news had arrived that Imam Hasan intended to make peace with Muawiya. Imam's friends were shocked at this unprecedented decision. Zayd's father was surprised as well, but his greater horror came when some of these companions began calling Imam Hasan a coward for choosing not to fight!

"Remember one thing, my dear Zayd," his mother would say. "Your Imam is your Imam whether he is sitting or standing; whether he calls you to fight or tells you to make peace." Little Zayd would nod his head solemnly. "People forgot this at Siffin with Imam Ali and paid greatly for it. They forgot again with Imam Hasan. God forbid if we betray another Imam…we may never be forgiven for our repeated disobedience!"

Zayd's father was aware of how difficult it was for Imam Hasan to make a treaty with a person like Muawiya. Even though he did not have the honour of fighting alongside his Imam, Zayd's father lived with the knowledge that his loyalty to Imam Hasan never wavered.

Despite Imam Hasan's effort to maintain peace within the ummah and bind the Umayyids to a semblance of Islamic practice, only days after the treaty was signed, Muawiya openly defied it. *I have put the treaty with Hasan ibn Ali under my two feet.*

Kufa had turned again. Imam Hasan left the city and Zayd's father was heartbroken. With every passing day, he became more restless. He could not stand by silently and watch people behave as if they had done nothing wrong. The last straw came when the then-ruler of Kufa, Ziad ibn Abiha, began to curse Imam Ali and Imam Hasan during the Friday sermon; his hatred for the Ahlulbayt fuelling his sharp tongue. Hujr ibn Adi stood up to protest this atrocity and Zayd's father eagerly joined in. They were both arrested along with a handful of supporters and sent to the court of Muawiya in Damascus.

The bad news came back a few weeks later. Zayd's mother and the families of those arrested heard that the prisoners had almost reached Damascus when the order was received for them to be mercilessly killed on the spot before having a chance to present their case before the court. They were all buried in the desert on the outskirts of Damascus.

****

Voices snap Zayd out of the memory that has swept him away into his past. The memories are comforting, but he needs to move and get to the tunnel gate. Every second spent in the open holds the risk of getting caught. He needs to be more alert. The voices are coming closer, and the reality of his situation amplifies the fear pulsing through his veins. Beads of sweat dot his forehead, his clammy skin a testament to the mounting terror that threatens to consume him. His fears are not unfounded. He peers around the corner and sees the group of men.

A few guards, but this time with armed soldiers! This is not a simple curfew survey; they seem to be a troop on a dedicated mission. Where are they headed at this hour? Zayd keeps hiding in the shadows craning his neck to follow their path. They stop in front of a house and bang on the door.

"Ibn Abi Ubayd! You are summoned by the Governor! Come out of the house in the name of the Caliph!"

They are at the doorstep of Mukhtar al Thaqafi! Everybody knows that he hosted Muslim ibn Aqeel when he first arrived in Kufa. The Governor must be hunting down those associated with Muslim; the threat against anyone who supports Husayn ibn Ali is extremely real and serious. The soldiers continue to bang on the door and when there is no response, they break it down without any hestitation.

"The house is empty! He has escaped!"

"Search the house again!"

"Spread out!"

"We must bring him to Ibn Ziyad, dead or alive!"

Zayd's heart begins to beat wildly out of control. He recalls the last meeting at Mukhtar's home when Muslim was alive and the pledges the people there had made.

By God, I will respond to you when you call upon me.

I will fight against your enemies.

I will strike my sword in your defence until I die.

I expect nothing more for this than God's pleasure.

All promises made to Ibn Aqeel barely a month ago and now the speakers of those words had either been killed, imprisoned, or cowed into silence. Conflicting thoughts run through Zayd's mind. Should he find Mukhtar and warn him? Should he continue to the tunnels?

Zayd's commitment to helping Imam Husayn is still intact. There is nothing he can do to help Mukhtar, and if he is caught then he will not be able to come to the aid of his Imam either. Once the soldiers spread out, the chance of being captured will increase tenfold. He must get to the entrance of the jinn tunnel as soon as possible.

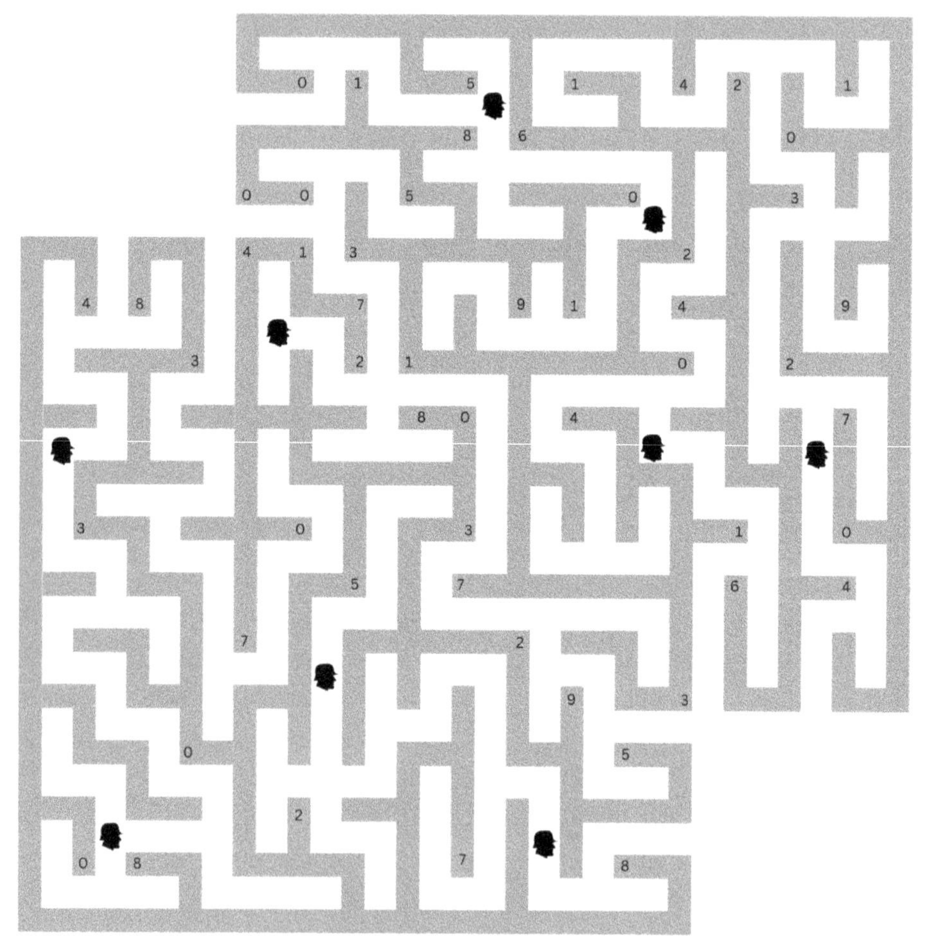

Zayd needs your help!

Find the solution to the code and write it in the box below. Then turn to that page number to continue the journey.

If you need some clues, go to page 129

THE OUTSKIRTS OF KUFA

Zayd lifts his head to check his surroundings. After miraculously—there is no other way to describe it—finding not one, but two stones that he could move, he has been able to break out of the tunnel and now finds himself against the outer wall of the city, gasping the clean, fresh cool night air in great gulps.

Now lying on the ground beneath the vast canopy of the night sky, he gathers his strength for whatever lies ahead. The darkness is beginning to lift ever so slightly, and he can just about see fragments of the surrounding landscape. This is the time when the faithful across Iraq will be waking up to communicate with their Lord in the sacred Tahajjud prayer. Zayd's communion with God this night involves a litany of pleas for guidance to reach his Imam. When he strains his eyes, he can just about make out the silhouettes of reeds and palms in the distance. He must be on the outer limits of Kufa. Reeds mean water will also be close by. His parched lips thirst for the life-giving drink, but he will need to cross the barren space ahead to reach the oasis.

***

The sand dunes and arid land ahead of him reminds Zayd of the plains of Arafat. After their first experience meeting Imam Hasan, Zayd's mother pledged to go for Hajj as often as she could. On one of those pilgrimages, Zayd remembers seeing Imam Husayn leave his tent in the heat of the Arafah afternoon. Even though he was covered in the same two simple white pieces of cloth as all the other pilgrims, the light on his face distinguished him from everyone around him.

He walked onto the open space, raised his palms in prayer, and began to supplicate aloud. Zayd was still a child then and was able to slip between the other pilgrims to come closer and hear the Imam's sweet whisperings of prayer. What would such a man say to his Lord?

If I pray to You, you will respond to me; and if I beg You, You will give me; And if I obey You, You will thank me and if I thank You, You will give me more....

Praise. Worship. Love.

Which of Your favours, my God, can I count in numbers and examples? Or which of Your gifts can I thank You for properly?

Thankfulness. Humility. So much Love.

You are my Haven when wild courses fail to carry me, and when the earth, despite its width, becomes too narrow to bear me...

Hope. Reliance. And Love...endless, infinite Love.

That was the day that it became as clear to him as the bright noon sun, that the family of the Prophet were not like other people. Zayd felt the presence of God flowing through his innocent self. Listening to Imam Husayn's supplication made him feel more alive than he had ever felt before. He had fallen in love with the God of Husayn and could not contain his yearning to know more, to learn more about his Lord. He had mustered the courage to go to Imam Husayn's tent where he found him standing and bowing, deep in prayer. *O Allah, show me the way to get close to You through this man.* The prayer had come from the depths of his heart.

Imam Husayn had turned around as if he had clearly heard the dua although Zayd had only whispered it under his breath. His kind eyes had a clear gaze and Zayd felt as if they were looking right into his soul. He gestured to Zayd to come closer and when the boy approached, he laid a gentle hand on his head, his eyes filled with tears of love.

"Our Lord ... is The One in Whose Kingdom everyone lives. Most of us worship Him, but few of us know Him. He is One but not in the sense of the number. He is the Hidden so that the probe of the wildest imaginations cannot grasp Him, and He is the Manifest in the way that all intellects can witness His presence."

Zayd watched the tears flowing freely down the Imam's cheeks, wetting his soft neat beard. He listened intently and tried to memorise the words; words whose meaning he could barely grasp, but whose message he knew would unfold for the rest of his life. This description of God was the one he turned to whenever he felt lonely in the years that followed.

"He is hidden but not absent; He is far but not distanced; He is close but not adjacent; He is intimate but not incarnate; He sees without means, hears without ears, plans without thought, and acts without organs. In His Dignity and with His Grace and Kindness, He has opened a window to our hearts to know Him and an impulse to thank Him and a love to praise Him. He is praised for what He is, praised for what He makes and praised for what He gives."

***

Zayd calms down as he recalls the peaceful memory and the powerful words. How can he ever thank the person who introduced him to God and taught him how to truly love his Creator? He wonders at the Umayyids and their supporters. Do they realise who they are attacking? Yes, they must, otherwise, they would not be so relentless.

Many had thought the Umayyids would leave Imam Hasan and his followers alone after the peace treaty. They were no longer a threat to their power...or were they? Muawiya had ordered Hujr ibn Adi and his companions, including Zayd's father, to be killed simply because they spoke out against the cursing of the Ahlulbayt, the Holy Household of the Prophet they all believed in and followed. Not satisfied with eliminating his supporters, Muawiya had finally poisoned Imam Hasan because he still felt intimidated by him. The Umayyids had even refused to allow Imam Hasan to be buried in peace.

Now, a decade later, the same hostility has risen against Imam Husayn. Zayd has heard the people of Kufa say that Imam Husayn should give allegiance to Yazid and save his own life. Don't they realise that Yazid will never leave him alone, no matter what he does?

Zayd has heard about Yazid's brutality and flagrant disregard for anything sanctified. Just remembering his name brings about a visceral reaction in him. He knows that Yazid, like his father Muawiya, will not be satisfied until he has spilt Imam Husayn's blood and the blood of anyone that supports him.

The thought of spilling the blood of the man who speaks to God with gentleness and love sends shivers through Zayd and fuels his determination. He looks out into the open plain once again and tries to estimate the distance. He whispers a prayer for his Imam's safety. What if he does not make it across? *Please Allah, help me to reach my Imam. I need to be with him!*

He wipes the wetness from his face. He has been weeping without even realising it. Desperation makes his chin quiver. As he rubs his eyes and clears his blurry vision, he notices fresh footprints in the sand. Someone has passed the same path he wants to and not too long ago. Was it a soldier? But what would a lone soldier be doing out here? Whoever it is, is headed towards the cluster of trees that Zayd wants to reach. Could it be another person trying to escape? Another person with a conscience heading out to help Imam Husayn! Zayd's spirits lift at the thought of another possible helper coming to the aid of Imam. Surely this must be a sign!

Zayd decides to place his trust in Allah and prepares to head towards the little grove that seems to be beckoning him to hurry up and reach the safety of its confines.

Zayd needs your help!

Find the solution to the code and write it in the box below. Then turn to that page number to continue the journey.

If you need some clues, go to page 131

THE FINAL ESCAPE

Zayd stands outside the tents watching the enemy. They are reciting the Fajr payers. Do they truly believe they praying to the God of Husayn? It seems impossible to believe that people can be so confused in their faith. Behind him, beautiful recitations of the Quran from the camp of Imam Husayn continue to fill the early morning desert air.

Once the sun rises, both armies prepare to battle. Imam Husayn positions the tents to protect the women and children. Zayd helps dig a trench around the tents. He fills it with firewood and sets it alight. The enemies will not be able to ambush the tents of the ladies while the men fight. A haunting realisation dawns over Zayd. What will the women and children do after all the man have all sacrificed their lives? Where will they go?

Zayd thinks of his own mother. What would she do if she were here with him? Her heart would break to see the lives of Lady Zainab and the other women of the Ahlulbayt in danger. It was Lady Zainab who had taught Zayd's mother how to recite and understand the Quran. Zayd knows she would have wanted to be here to support and help. *Let my sacrifice be on her behalf*, he prays. I would not be here if it were not for her upbringing.

His thoughts are interrupted by the sound of galloping hooves. Imam Husayn has mounted a camel and, accompanied by a couple of his companions, is heading out to the enemy ranks. He stops in the land between them, in what will be the battleground for the day, and faces the tens of thousands of heavily armed men. The battle drums stop beating and silence falls on both sides until there is not a single sound to be heard. Even the horses seem to be holding their breath.

When Imam Husayn speaks, his voice rings clear and true across the desert sands. He tries to reason with the enemy. He reminds them of who he is, reminds them of their own humanity. He asks the Kufans to recall the hundreds of letters they had written to him.

To Zayd, he seems to be a kind father offering advice to misguided children. But it is to no avail. They are not listening. Some cover their ears with their hands, others begin to clash their swords on their shields to drown out the Imam's speech and soon there is chaos and he can no longer be heard. He stops speaking and turns back. It seems to Zayd that Imam is more grieved on behalf of the enemy than on what awaits them. He can tell that bloodshed is inevitable. The enemy is shouting that they will not rest until they have spilled the blood of the grandson of the Prophet. *Not whilst I am alive, you won't*, Zayd thinks. *Not whilst I breathe and can defend him.*

He buckles borrowed armour plates to his chest and legs. They are too big for him, but he knows he will not need them for long. Coming to terms with his own end has not been as hard as he thought it would be. He is on the brink of martyrdom and success has been promised by Imam Husayn himself. What more can he want? He whispers a prayer that he heard earlier from the Imam:

O God, I put my trust in You in every tribulation.

You are my Hope in every distress.

An arrow flies through the air and lands in front of Imam Husayn's camp.

"Bear witness that I was the first to strike!" cries a voice from behind enemy lines. It is Umar ibn Sa'ad.

Death is now visible on the horizon and Zayd knows it is just a matter of waiting. He can count the number of times he has carried a sword, and he has never used one on another person. But if anyone dares to try and harm his Imam, he is ready to cut the attacker to pieces. Keeping his eyes fixed on the enemy soldiers, he tightens his turban around his head. His ankle throbs as he mounts the horse but his breath is steady. One more march forward. One more burst of courage. One last time.

After the morning battle, their numbers have dwindled, but Zayd is still alive. One-on-one combat begins in the afternoon and within an hour, the burning sand is filled with corpses whose colour have changed because of death and loss of blood. Zayd awaits his turn to prove himself and tries not to be scared. He thinks of his father, standing at sunrise in a strange town fifty miles from Damascus; he imagines him hearing the order for execution. Was he frightened? Did he tremble as Zayd is now?

The sun continues to unrelentingly scorch down upon them, as if protesting the injustice it is being forced to witness. Zayd looks to Imam Husayn for permission; it is finally his turn to fight. He urges his horse forward onto the battlefield, adrenaline pumping through his body.

He is being fuelled by a force beyond his own capacity and the words of war-poetry spill from his lips unbidden.

"I am the son of the one killed for his love of Hasan ibn Ali,

I escaped from Kufa, and with Husayn I am free,

Before you can get to him, you will have to go through me,

For I will not live knowing Husayn's life is in jeopardy!"

A soldier twice his age approaches from enemy lines. He smiles crookedly. "I warned you about your death, boy," he says. Zayd recognises him as the man who chased him while he ran towards the camp of Imam Husayn.

Thinking Zayd is an easy target, he attacks openly, swiping his sword straight at his neck. Zayd raises his weapon quickly, blocking the attack. The clash of swords rings out. The soldier tries again with a more powerful swing, but he has not accounted for Zayd's youthful agility. Zayd ducks, leaving his opponent off balance. He uses the chance to strike at the soldier's chest whilst the man's arms are flailing for balance. Zayd's sharp sword pierces through the armour and the soldier falls to the ground. Zayd is shocked. Is he dead? He scans the ground around him to find where he fell, but he cannot see a body. Before he can think, Zayd is being yanked from his horse by hands he cannot see.

He hits the ground, and his helmet is knocked off from the impact of his head on the ground. The soldier places a heavy knee on his chest constricting his breathing. Zayd gropes for his sword whilst gasping for breath. His fingers brush the hilt and he grasps it with one hand, using the other to try and hold the soldier back. The sword is heavy in his hand, but with a shout of *Allahu Akbar!* he manages to lift it and push the blade through the side of the soldier's chest. The soldier stops and shudders. His eyes widen in shock as his sword falls from his hand. Disbelief is written all over his face as he looks down and then collapses half-conscious on top of Zayd.

Pinned under the weight of the man and his armour, Zayd can neither move nor breathe. As he struggles to free himself, he realizes the man is not dead yet. The soldier reaches for something in his boot and when he raises his arm, a short, sharp, serrated blade glints in the sun. Zayd tries to move his arms to grab a hold of the soldier's wrist but they are pinned down by the soldier's knees. His breath slows down and he watches as if in slow motion as the man raises the blade higher and then brings it down with all his might to thrust the dagger deep into Zayd's heart.

A moment of intense pain, followed by a sudden relief and a sense of clarity. The blinding sun, the burning sand, his parched throat and the smell of sweat and blood all fade away in an instant. Zayd sees his father walking towards him in a silver robe, arms outstretched to welcome him.

"Congratulations, my son, you have escaped the attachments of this world. Enter the paradise that awaits you."

يَـٰٓأَيَّتُهَا ٱلنَّفْسُ ٱلْمُطْمَئِنَّةُ

ٱرْجِعِىٓ إِلَىٰ رَبِّكِ رَاضِيَةً مَّرْضِيَّةً

فَٱدْخُلِى فِى عِبَـٰدِى

وَٱدْخُلِى جَنَّتِى

THE EUPHRATES

Zayd hears the gentle burbling of the water and smells its clean earthy scent before he sees it. He quickens his steps. Relief. He has finally found it! He pushes past the final reeds to reveal the sparkling river flowing across his path. Zayd half-stumbles, half-crawls and using the final dregs of his vitality hurls himself into the flowing waters of the Euphrates. The cold hits him like a wall. It feels like his entire body is being stabbed by needles of ice. He has never felt so much physical pain in his entire life. He has no energy left to fight, he lets his body float and allows the water to run around him, over him, through him. He imagines it washing away all the blood and sweat, all the venom and tears.

As the seconds flow past, the intense agony fades aways gradually until Zayd is left bobbing along in the quiet waters, numb of any pain for the first time that night. He feels a sense of peace, a foreign feeling that he hasn't felt for a long time. The sky above him is visibly lightening, it is time for the dawn prayer. He has made it! Haarith's house, Ibn Ziyad's palace, the treacherous streets of Kufa and the predators of the night-forest are now behind him. It feels like years have passed between last night and this morning. He turns and swims to the bank, pulling himself out of the river. He is sore but feeling much better. He cups some water in his palm and drinks it, revelling in the sweet, fresh taste. Never has ordinary water tasted so good! After quenching his thirst, he performs wudhu and stands for fajr prayer.

Allahu Akbar – God is the Greatest.

The motions of prayer revive him. He thanks God for making it this far and prays for strength to continue. When he completes his prayer, he looks around. He needs to join Imam Husayn, but which way should he go? The desert is so vast, if he sets out in the wrong direction, he could end up going further away from his goal. Sitting facing the qibla, he seeks direction from God.

You are hidden but not absent, far but not distanced.

You are my Hope, You are my Guide...

He stares at the flowing river, the ripples and eddies entrancing him. The early morning light filtering through the trees bounces off its surface, scattering like diamond dust. It is so calm and yet so full of life. Something strange catches his attention: a large piece of driftwood floating upstream. Tree branches often fall into the river or it could be a piece of a broken vessel. Zayd's mind begins to race.

A boat would be the fastest and safest way to cross the desert. Guards are usually restricted to cities and do not patrol the water's edge. Imam Husayn was last known to be coming towards Kufa and he will be sure to keep near water, so if Zayd paddles upstream against the current, he might come across someone who will know where Imam has camped! Besides, travelling on land will be slow and difficult with his ankle; he will be able to cover a greater distance in the water.

Zayd hobbles to the edge of the water and jumps in to catch the driftwood before it passes. His lips set in a firm line; he is ready for the next step in his journey. Bismillah! He presses his palms onto the rough wood and pulls himself aboard.

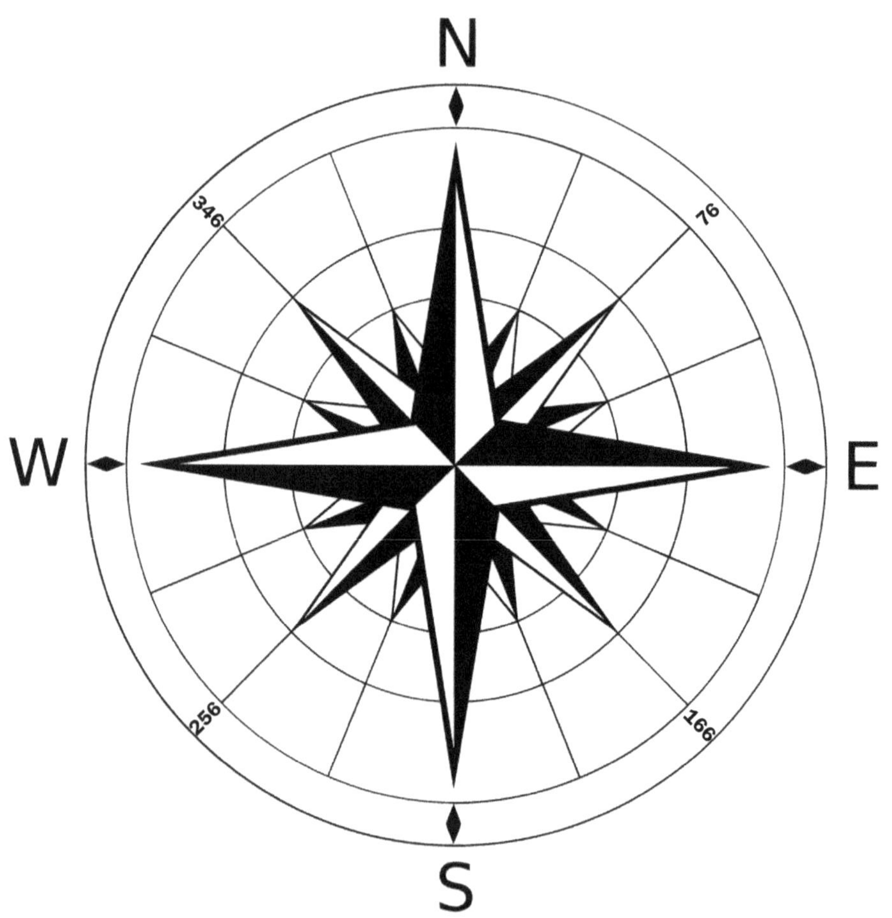

N
76
E
166
S
256
W
346

Zayd needs your help!

Find the solution to the code and write it in the box below. Then turn to that page number to continue the journey.

If you need some clues, go to page 133

THE FOREST

Fifty metres.

Zayd runs as fast as he can. The wind whips the loose end of his turban across his shoulders.

Forty metres.

His chest is burning with the strain. He is pushing his body past its limits, but still he runs.

Thirty metres.

Run away from Kufans and their hypocrisy. Run away from the power-hungry cowards. Run away from Ibn Ziyad and his threats.

Zayd pushes forward, leaning into the cool air, panting, gasping, flailing, but never faltering.

Twenty metres.

He gathers his final burst of willpower.

Run towards Husayn. Run towards success. Run towards...

He doesn't know what he will find when he reaches Imam Husayn...if he reaches Imam Husayn.

Zayd's mind is a whirlwind of tangled thoughts. He knows that Imam Husayn is in real danger. He knows what the Ummayids are capable of. They are an unscrupulous clan given to threatening, bribing, and killing to get what they want. They broke the peace treaty with Imam Hasan, turned his supporters against him and manipulated others to murder him. Zayd knows them. He studies them. He gets their way, and he knows that they will not stop until they have got rid of each and every member of the Ahlulbayt; so threatened by their very existence, he now knows with all certainty that they will no longer hide their hatred for Imam Husayn. Clarity pierces his thoughts and Zayd runs with determination towards the forest.

The last ten metres.

He lets himself imagine what it will feel like to greet Imam Husayn and place his hand in his. To stand alongside Abul Fadhl Abbas, Ali Akbar and the other young Hashimite men — that is all that matters now. Adrenaline pumps through his veins and Zayd hurls himself into the trees with a final burst of energy.

He falls onto the bed of cool grass, damp with dew. Slumped face down on the ground, he pants in shallow breaths and waits for the loud thundering beat of his heart to fade from his eardrums. The wet grass provides some relief to his dry lips, moistening them with the precious liquid. After endless moments, he drags himself to the base of a nearby palm tree and sits with his back against its trunk. Has he really made it? His uncle's cellar, the tension-laden streets of Kufa, the dank passage under the city...it all feels like a dream now, memories from a distant past. He is here finally, free from Kufa and its curfew. For the moment, under the cover of the forest, he is safe. He allows relief to wash over his body and releases the tension he had gathered from his shoulders. His breathing slows.

There are large, feathery fronds and springy reeds around him. He appreciates the camouflage and nestles into the blanket of soft grass, finally letting his guard down. Exhaustion overtakes him and he allows his eyes to close.

Just for a moment... he promises himself.

Zayd needs your help!

Find the solution to the code and write it in the box below. Then turn to that page number to continue the journey.

If you need some clues, go to page 135

THE LAST NIGHT

When Zayd opens his eyes, he is laying on a pallet inside a large tent. Zayd blinks to clear his vision. The tent is full of men, but it is calm. Zayd looks around; these man remind him of his father. A soft hum of gentle voices contrast the loud shouting and music from Umar ibn Sa'ad's camp.

Umar ibn Sa'ad! Zayd jolts back to reality.

He remembers Ibn Sa'ad riding out to confront Imam Husayn's camp. Have they started to attack already? His eyes dart across the tent, looking for a familiar face. He spots Habib ibn Mazahir sitting to one side, sharpening his sword. Zayd can hardly believe his eyes. Habib was still in Kufa when Muslim ibn Aqeel and Hani ibn Urwah were murdered by Ibn Ziyad. How did he reach here? Zayd recalls the footsteps he had seen along his way and wonders if they belonged to Habib.

"Shaykh..." He calls out. "You are here. You escaped Kufa as well?"

Habib look up at Zayd's call. He smiles. "Where Husayn goes, Habib will follow."

Zayd sits up and warns him. "The enemy is planning to attack today! We must prepare ourselves."

"Imam Husayn has asked for one more night," Habib reassures him.

One more night? Zayd is confused. What difference will that make? What can happen overnight to change the dire situation they are in?

Habib smiles again. He seems to be able to hear the questions running through Zayd's mind. "It is one more night for us to pray and recite the Quran," he explains softly.

Zayd watches in wonder as the men around him immerse themselves in prayer and reciting the Quran. The tents are filled with the hum of dhikr and tasbeeh as each faithful companion seeks to taste the sweetness of communication with their Lord. The atmosphere is electric. Zayd cannot believe how calm the men around him are. They are aware of the thousands of bloodthirsty soldiers waiting for them the following day, and yet they talk and joke with each other as if they were on a journey of leisure. Some of them even seem excited at the prospect of what awaits them. This is the effect of true trust and faith in God.

Later in the night, Imam Husayn gathers his companions and Zayd sits amongst them, feeding off their infectious fervour. What advice will Imam Husayn give them? There is silence as they all wait to hear the words of the Prophet's grandson.

"I believe tomorrow will be our last day that will be brought about by these enemies," the Imam tells them. He looks keenly at each person before him. "I have given thought to your situation."

What is Imam Husayn going to say? Zayd holds his breath. He seems to be speaking directly to each of their hearts. He pauses slightly and then continues.

"You are absolved of your obligation to me," he says. "If you wish to, you are justified to leave."

Murmurs fill the camp and the companions look at each other in disbelief. No one seems to know how to respond.

"Use this cover of night to escape."

Escape? Zayd thinks about that word. He does not want to escape anymore. He has spent the past twenty-four hours escaping everything else that stood in his way just to arrive here! This is the only place he wants to be — with Imam Husayn. Now, Zayd finally has a purpose and meaning in life.

Imam Husayn continues to speak, but Zayd is distracted by his thoughts. Suddenly he hears Abul Fadhl speak up. "Why would we ever do that? In order to remain alive after you? May God never allow that to happen."

The family of the Prophet and Imam Husayn's companions all echo Abbas's words and Zayd joins in. He hears himself promise never to leave Imam Husayn, even if it means sacrificing his life, and realises that he means every single word. He cannot imagine his life beyond that of Imam Husayn's. He will never return to Kufa. He will do what his father didnt get a chance to: he will fight alongside his Imam.

Muslim ibn Awsajah stands up. "How is it possible to leave you and then hold before God that we had fulfilled your rights? By God, I will not do so until I have thrust my spear into their chests, and smitten them with my sword until only its hilt remains in my hand. I will not leave you. If I have no weapon with which to fight them, I will hurl stones at them to secure your safety until I die with you."

Zuhayr ibn Qayn says, "By God, I would love to be killed, then revived, then killed a thousand times in this manner—if it would keep you safe with the young ones from your family."

Zayd thinks about his journey so far and about being killed a thousand times again. Can he make the same claim as Zuhayr? Yes. The answer comes clear and without hesitation. Yes! He would do this for Husayn. Never in his life has he felt so much love for a person. He is prepared to die.

بِسْمِ اللَّهِ الرَّحْمَٰنِ الرَّحِيمِ

وَالسَّمَاءِ ذَاتِ الْبُرُوجِ ﴿١﴾ وَالْيَوْمِ الْمَوْعُودِ ﴿٢﴾ وَشَاهِدٍ وَمَشْهُودٍ ﴿٣﴾ قُتِلَ أَصْحَابُ الْأُخْدُودِ ﴿٤﴾ النَّارِ ذَاتِ الْوَقُودِ ﴿٥﴾ إِذْ هُمْ عَلَيْهَا قُعُودٌ ﴿٦﴾ وَهُمْ عَلَىٰ مَا يَفْعَلُونَ بِالْمُؤْمِنِينَ شُهُودٌ ﴿٧﴾ وَمَا نَقَمُوا مِنْهُمْ إِلَّا أَن يُؤْمِنُوا بِاللَّهِ الْعَزِيزِ الْحَمِيدِ ﴿٨﴾ الَّذِي لَهُ مُلْكُ السَّمَاوَاتِ وَالْأَرْضِ ۚ وَاللَّهُ عَلَىٰ كُلِّ شَيْءٍ شَهِيدٌ ﴿٩﴾ إِنَّ الَّذِينَ فَتَنُوا الْمُؤْمِنِينَ وَالْمُؤْمِنَاتِ ثُمَّ لَمْ يَتُوبُوا فَلَهُمْ عَذَابُ جَهَنَّمَ وَلَهُمْ عَذَابُ الْحَرِيقِ ﴿١٠﴾ إِنَّ الَّذِينَ آمَنُوا وَعَمِلُوا الصَّالِحَاتِ لَهُمْ جَنَّاتٌ تَجْرِي مِن تَحْتِهَا الْأَنْهَارُ ۚ ذَٰلِكَ الْفَوْزُ الْكَبِيرُ ﴿١١﴾ إِنَّ بَطْشَ رَبِّكَ لَشَدِيدٌ ﴿١٢﴾ إِنَّهُ هُوَ يُبْدِئُ وَيُعِيدُ ﴿١٣﴾ وَهُوَ الْغَفُورُ الْوَدُودُ ﴿١٤﴾ ذُو الْعَرْشِ الْمَجِيدُ ﴿١٥﴾ فَعَّالٌ لِّمَا يُرِيدُ ﴿١٦﴾ هَلْ أَتَاكَ حَدِيثُ الْجُنُودِ ﴿١٧﴾ فِرْعَوْنَ وَثَمُودَ ﴿١٨﴾ بَلِ الَّذِينَ كَفَرُوا فِي تَكْذِيبٍ ﴿١٩﴾ وَاللَّهُ مِن وَرَائِهِم مُّحِيطٌ ﴿٢٠﴾ بَلْ هُوَ قُرْآنٌ مَّجِيدٌ ﴿٢١﴾ فِي لَوْحٍ مَّحْفُوظٍ ﴿٢٢﴾

Zayd needs your help!

Find the solution to the code and write it in the box below. Then turn to that page number to continue the journey.

If you need some clues, go to page 137

CLUES AND SOLUTIONS

THE CELLAR

Clue 1:

The code lies where the footholds do not.

Clue 2:

Two numbers are hidden on the wall.

Clue 3:

Trace the area without footholds with your finger to find the outline of the numbers.

Clue 4:

There is one number on the top half of the wall and another number on the bottom half of the wall.

ANSWER = 67

UMAR IBN SA'AD'S TENT

Clue 1:

The code is at the entrance of the tent

Clue 2:

Most of the numbers are insignificant. Only two of them are important.

Clue 3:

To find the two numbers that are important, you need to fold the paper.

Clue 4:

Fold the paper into two triangles to make a tent.

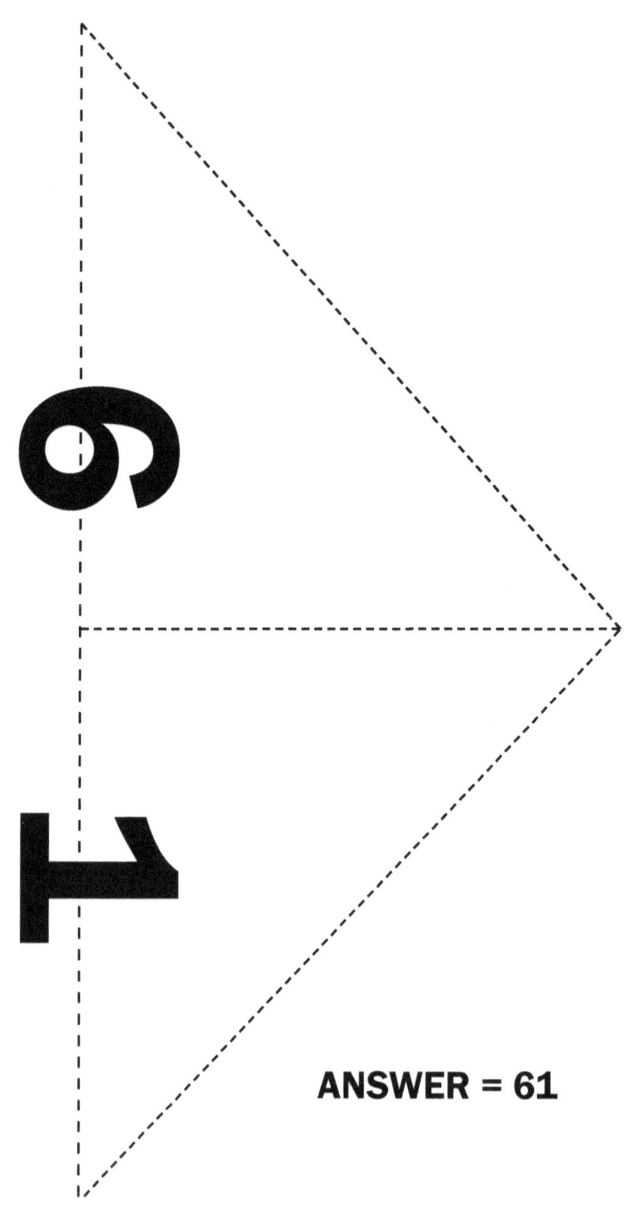

ANSWER = 61

WAKE UP ZAYD!

Clue 1:

The verse at the end of the chapter is significant.

Clue 2:

The code is hidden in the sky.

Clue 3:

One number is hidden on the left page and the other on the right page. The code reads from left to right.

Clue 4:

Hold the book close to your nose, focus in and then slowly move it away as if you are looking past the picture.

ANSWER = 43

SOLDIERS

Clue 1:

You need to use the camera app on your phone to unlock the code.

Clue 2:

Visit https://www.sunbehindthecloud.com/first-escape-book

Clue 3:

The numbers in the sequence are:

625, 529, 441, 361, 289, 225, 169, 121, 81, ?

Clue 4:

The numbers are square numbers.

25	25 × 25	625
24	24 × 24	576
23	23 × 23	529
22	22 × 22	484
21	21 × 21	441
20	20 × 20	400
19	19 × 19	361
18	18 × 18	324
17	17 × 17	289
16	16 × 16	256
15	15 × 15	225
14	14 × 14	196
13	13 × 13	169
12	12 × 12	144
11	11 × 11	121
10	10 × 10	100
9	9 × 9	81
8	8 × 8	64
7	7 × 7	<u>49</u>

ANSWER = 49

INSIDE THE TUNNEL

Clue 1:

There are two blocks that are loose.

Clue 2:

Find two numbers in the wall of zeros.

Clue 3:

One of the numbers is on the left page and the other is on the right.

Clue 4:

The order of the code reads from left to right.

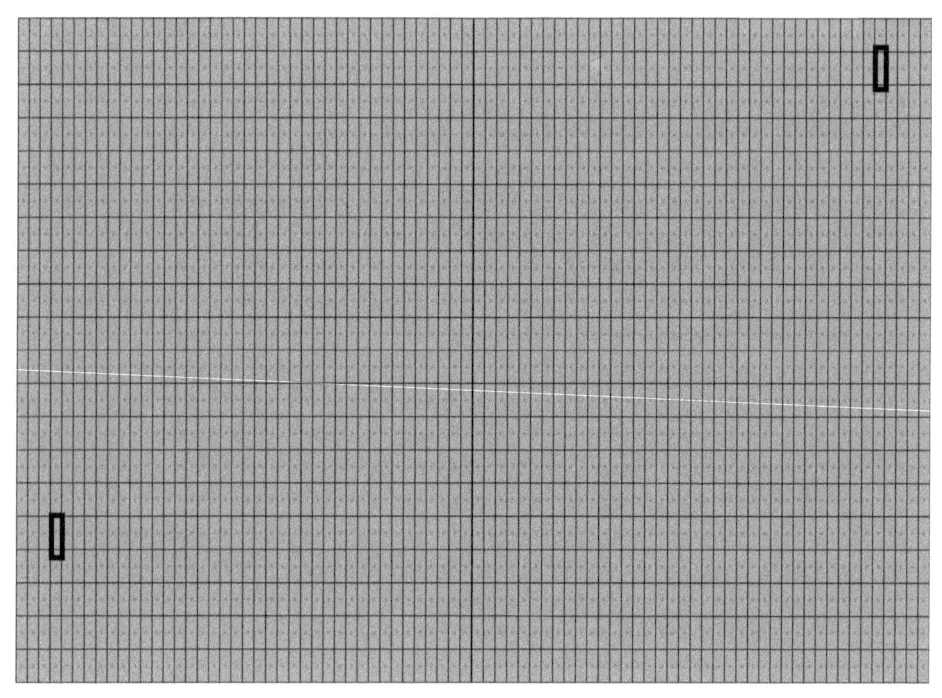

ANSWER = 77

THE MOTHER BIRD

Clue 1:

Re-read the chapter and find the path that the bird takes.

Clue 2:

she hops over a leaf, climbs carefully up a twig, and then jumps over a flower...

Clue 3:

Start in the top left corner.

Clue 4:

There are two paths that will lead to two numbers. The code reads from top to bottom.

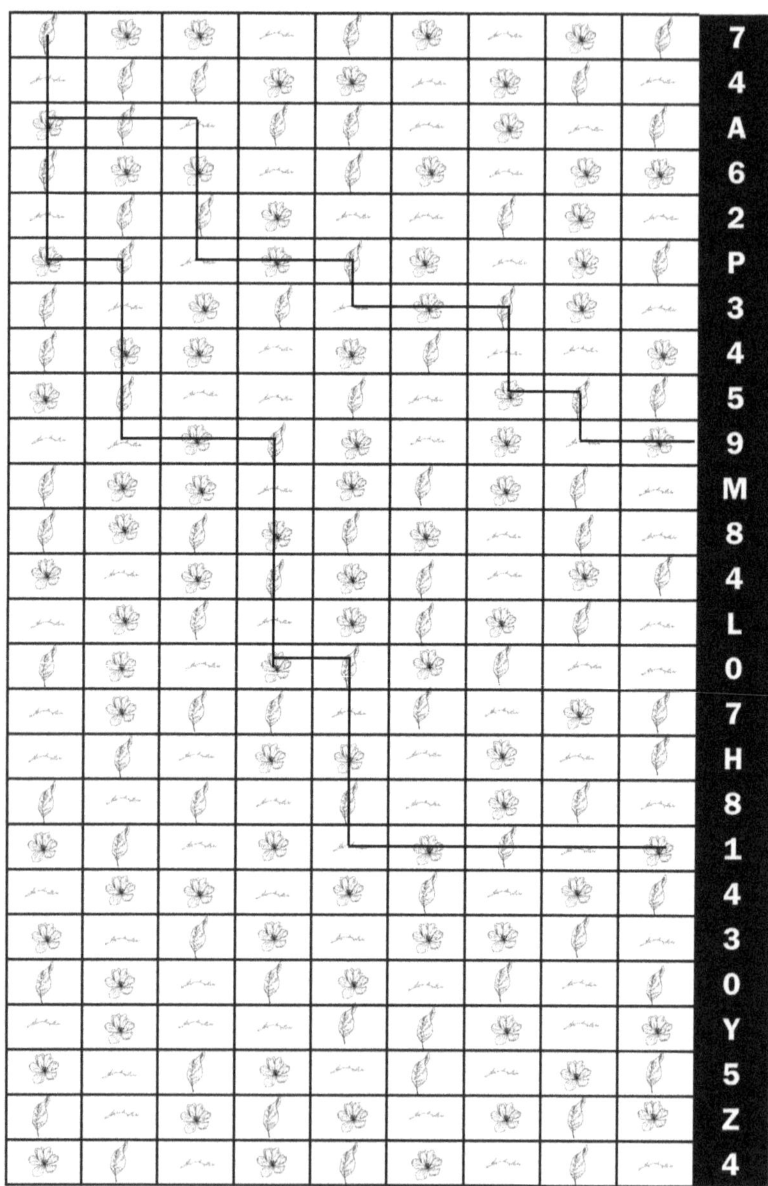

ANSWER= 91

THE ENEMY CAMP

Clue 1:

The letters in the grid make up a phrase.

Clue 2:

The first word of the phrase begins on the top row, second letter in.

Clue 3:

The letters in the phrase go down and across. No diagonals.

Clue 4:

The beginning of the phrase you are looking for is:

Follow the path to the code...

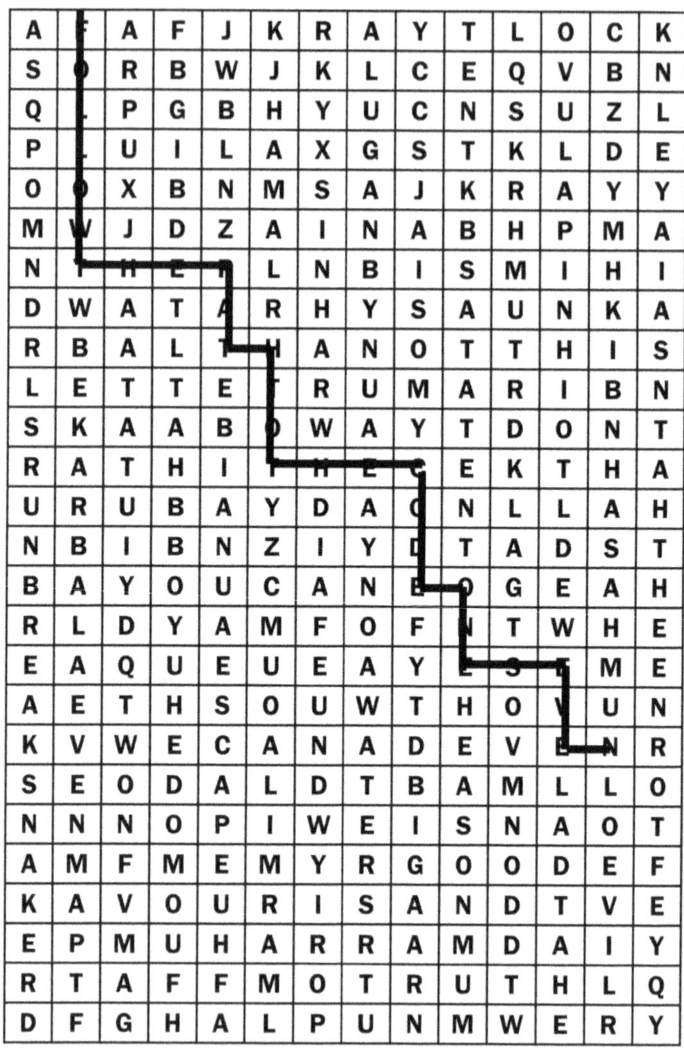

ANSWER = 17

ACCESSING THE TUNNEL

Clue 1:

Begin by decoding the letters at the top. The words are written without spaces and the starting point is the same as in Arabic.

Clue 2:

The phrase says:

To find the code turn the handle three times

Clue 3:

The first cog turns clockwise.

Clue 4:

The code reads from top to bottom.

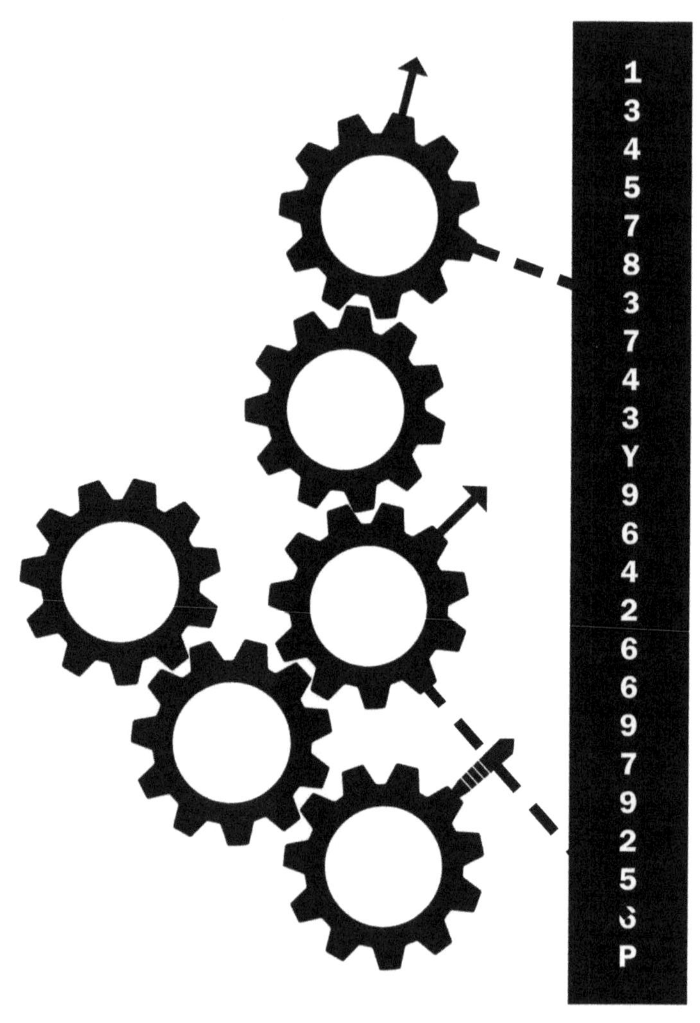

ANSWER = 36

REACHING IMAM HUSAYN

Clue 1:

Arabic numerals are used.

Clue 2:

The puzzle is solved from the top left quadrant, working clockwise.

Clue 3:

The numbers on the outer quadrants affect the inner quadrants.

Clue 4:

The numbers in the inner quadrants are cumulative.

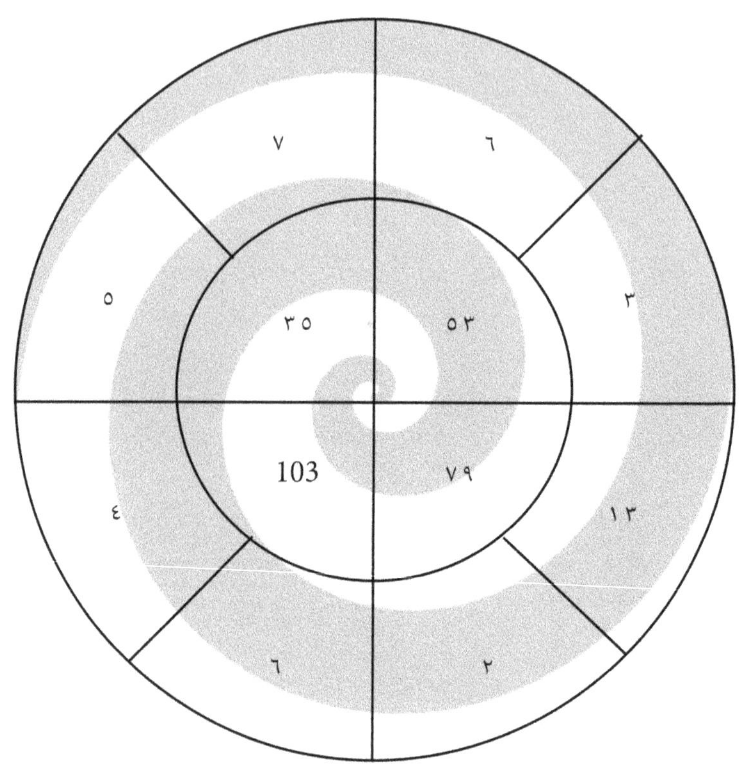

5 x 7 = 35
6 x 3 =18
13 x 2 = 26
6 x 4 = 24
35 + 18 + 26 + 24 = 103
ANSWER = 103

THE STREETS OF KUFA

Clue 1:

Find your way through the maze avoiding the soldiers and dead ends.

Clue 2:

The numbers on the path are significant.

Clue 3:

Add the numbers on both sides of the path to reach the solution.

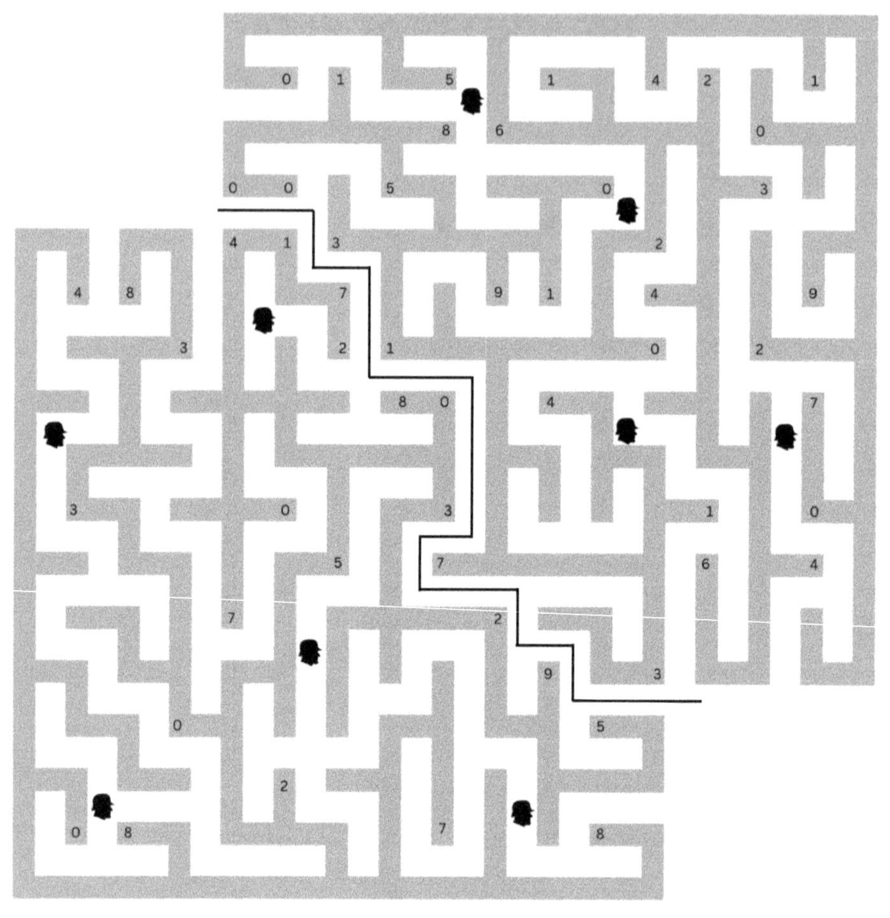

$$4+1+3+7+2+1+8+3+7+2+9+5+3=55$$

ANSWER = 55

THE OUTSKIRTS OF KUFA

Clue 1:

The footsteps are in a grid.

Clue 2:

Read the grid as you would a map.

Clue 3:

Along the corridor and up the stairs.

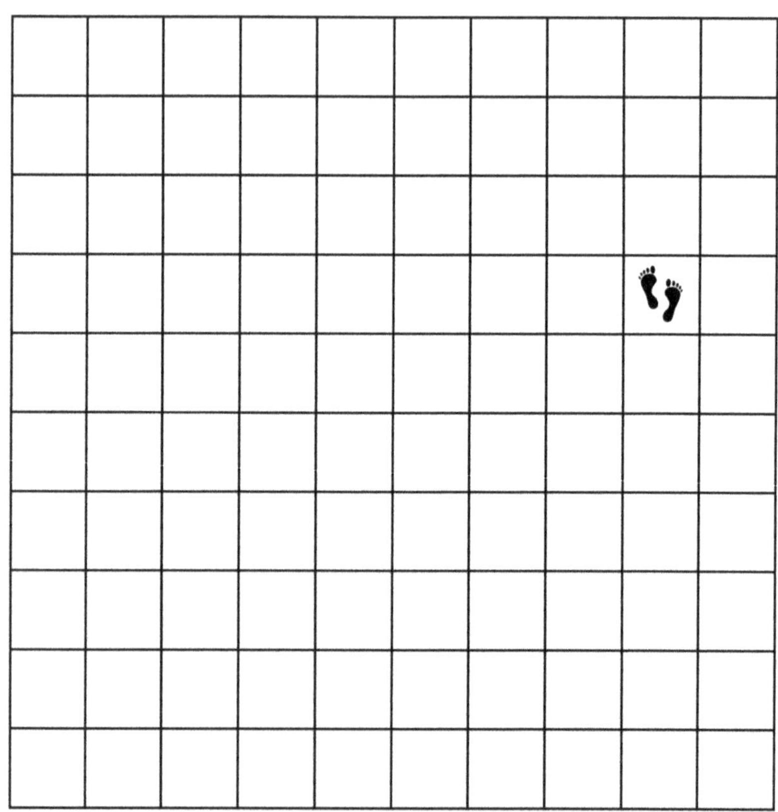

THE COORDINATES ARE 9,7
ANSWER = 97

THE EUPHRATES

Clue 1:

When Zayd is asking God for direction, he sees a piece of driftwood floating upstream.

Clue 2:

The Euphrates flows from Kufa to Kerbala.

Clue 3:

Kerbala is north of Kufa.

Clue 4:

76-45=

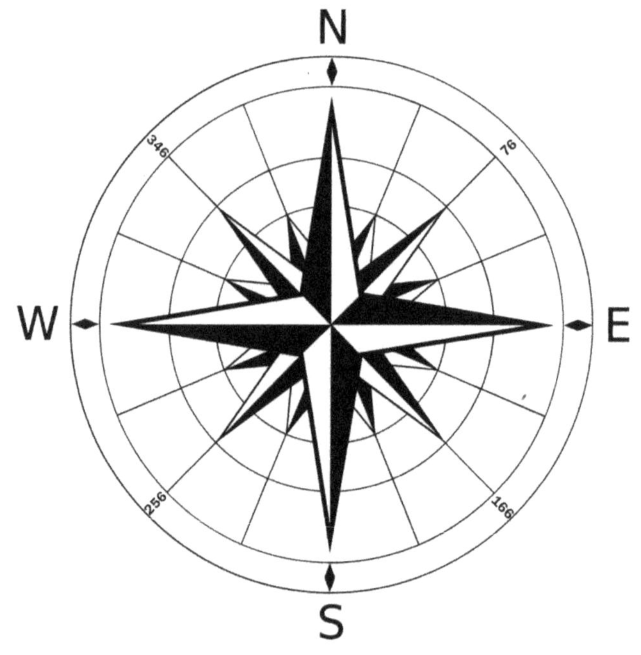

NORTH - 31 DEGREES
ANSWER = 31

THE FOREST

Clue 1:

Zayd must reach the forest of reeds and palms.

Clue 2:

He must run a distance to get there.

Clue 3:

Measure the distance with a ruler.

24cm

SOLUTION NOT TO SCALE
ANSWER = 24

THE LAST NIGHT

Clue 1:

Imam Husayn and his companions spent their last night reading the Quran.

Clue 2:

Does this surah look familiar?

Clue 3:

There is a question mark where there is something missing on the page.

Clue 4:

The question mark is where the surah number should be.

SURAH BURUJ IS THE 85TH SURAH IN THE QURAN.

ANSWER = 85.

www.ingramcontent.com/pod-product-compliance
Lightning Source LLC
Chambersburg PA
CBHW040538170726
48295CB00012B/509